*Elizabeth is about to catch
Sam in a very big lie. . . .*

"Excuse me," Elizabeth said to the clerk behind the desk at the Sweet Valley Resort Hotel. "I asked for Sam Burgess's room, but I was sent to a room with a plaque on the door that says Owner's Suite. There must be some mistake."

The clerk raised an eyebrow. "You did say you were looking for Mr. Burgess, did you not?"

"Yes, *Sam* Burgess," Elizabeth clarified.

"Sam Burgess owns the hotel," the clerk said.

"*Owns* the hotel?" Elizabeth could barely contain her disbelief.

The clerk sighed. "That is why Mr. Burgess is in the *owner's suite*."

"Wait a second. Are we talking about the same Mr. Sam Burgess here? The one I'm looking for is nineteen years old, sandy brown hair, dressed like a college student, probably wearing jeans and a T-shirt?"

"Yes, that's him," the clerk answered slowly, as if speaking to a child.

Huh? Elizabeth thought. *Could there be two Sam Burgesses that match that description?*

There was only one way to find out.

Bantam Books in the Sweet Valley University series.
Ask your bookseller for the books you have missed.

And don't miss these Sweet Valley
University Thriller Editions:

Visit the Official Sweet Valley Web Site on the Internet at:

http://www.sweetvalley.com

SWEET VALLEY UNIVERSITY®

Who Knew?

**Written by
Laurie John**

**Created by
FRANCINE PASCAL**

BANTAM BOOKS
NEW YORK • TORONTO • LONDON • SYDNEY • AUCKLAND

RL: 8, AGES 014 AND UP

WHO KNEW?
A Bantam Book / May 2000

Sweet Valley High® *and Sweet Valley University*®
are registered trademarks of Francine Pascal.
Conceived by Francine Pascal.

Produced by 17th Street Productions,
an Alloy Online, Inc. company.
33 West 17th Street
New York, NY 10011.

ISBN: 0-553-49309-4

Visit us on the Web! www.randomhouse.com/teens

Published simultaneously in the United States and Canada

Bantam Books is an imprint of Random House Children's Books, a
division of Random House, Inc. BANTAM BOOKS and the rooster
colophon are registered trademarks of Random House, Inc. Bantam Books,
1540 Broadway, New York, New York 10036.

PRINTED IN THE UNITED STATES OF AMERICA

OPM   0 9 8 7 6 5 4 3 2 1

To Grant Linville Hyvn

Chapter One

I'm not in my own bed, Elizabeth Wakefield realized dimly the moment she opened her eyes.

The scratchy sheet, thin, plaid comforter, and hard-as-a-rock pillow were nothing like the soft, pretty bedding in her attic room. The lumpy mattress sagged in the middle, unlike her firm Sealy. And the faint smell of T-shirts that needed to be washed was very different from the scented potpourri Elizabeth kept on her bedside table.

No, she thought, bolting upright in the narrow bed. *I definitely didn't sleep in my room last night.* She glanced down at herself; she was fully dressed in a tank top and sweats.

The door suddenly flew open. "Listen, Sam, I'm so pissed at—"

The angry voice of her twin sister, Jessica, stopped midsentence. Jessica stared at Elizabeth,

1

her mouth hanging open, her eyes narrowed.

"You're so pissed at Sam *because* . . ." Elizabeth prompted, hoping that Jessica was too half awake and in need of coffee to notice that Elizabeth had clearly just woken up in Sam Burgess's bed.

But from the looks of Jessica in a fitness bra, shorts, running shoes, ponytail, and sweatband, her sister was uncharacteristically wide awake at 8:30 A.M.—and about to go for a run.

"And you slept in Sam's bed *because* . . ." Jessica asked in the same prompting tone. "*Omigod.*" Jessica looked behind her, then shut the door and rushed inside. She perched next to Elizabeth and grabbed her arm. "Did you and Sam—"

Elizabeth almost laughed. "Do you *see* him anywhere? It would be difficult to have sex with a guy who didn't come home last night. And Jess, trust me, if I ever lose my virginity, you'll be the second person to know."

That seemed to shut up her sister for the moment. Elizabeth took the time to stare out the window. *Where is Sam?* she wondered for the hundredth time since Thursday morning.

Elizabeth knew that Sam was avoiding her. He'd been avoiding her for days now, ever since they had kissed very unexpectedly on Wednesday night.

One kiss. One not-so-simple kiss had sent him packing and running.

Jessica let out an exaggerated breath. "Whew! I am majorly relieved. For a second there I thought my worst nightmare had come true: that you and Mr. Commitment-phobic actually hooked up and became a couple!"

Elizabeth gnawed at her lower lip. *That* was exactly what she *wanted* to happen. What she thought *had* happened on Wednesday night.

Jessica tightened her ponytail, then stood up and headed into the kitchen, which opened from Sam's room. Elizabeth heard the sounds of a cabinet opening and mugs clinking.

"So why *did* you sleep in his room?" Jessica called as she poured fresh-brewed coffee into two mugs.

Elizabeth peeled off the comforter, stood, and stretched her cramped muscles. She followed her sister into the kitchen. "I, uh, I wanted to talk to him about something important, so I was, um, waiting for him to come home." Elizabeth wasn't about to tell her sister that her biggest nightmare *had* sort of come true.

Jessica handed Elizabeth a mug of steaming, much needed coffee, then sat down on a stool at the table. "Liz, spill it. Now. Not the coffee— *what's* going on with you and Sam?"

Elizabeth sat down at the table across from her sister. "There's stuff you don't know, okay?"

Jessica raised an eyebrow. "Like what?"

There was so much she hadn't told Jessica, Elizabeth realized. "Like the night that Finn threw me out of his apartment because I wouldn't sleep with him." As Finn Robinson's gorgeous face floated momentarily in Elizabeth's mind, she couldn't believe she'd once thought herself in love with the SVU med student. Or that she'd fallen for his lies. "Sam came and got me, and I was such a mess. Sam was *totally* there for me—that night and the next few days. So, I'm sort of pro-Sam these days, Jess."

Jessica's expression softened. "Look, Liz, I know Finn hurt you bad—I wish I could undo everything that jerk put you through. But trust me, Sam *isn't* your friend, okay? I'm sure all he's been doing is gloating. He kept insisting Finn was slime, and he turned out to be right. Sam Burgess doesn't care about anyone but himself. You know it as well as I do. In fact, you know it better than *anyone*."

Elizabeth knew her sister was referring to what had happened between her and Sam last summer, when they'd met. She and Sam had hooked up briefly, but they'd split up as friends. Elizabeth had been hurt, but not heartbroken. What *had* been heartbreaking was the way he hadn't kept in touch at all after the summer. He'd ignored Elizabeth's letters, and she probably wouldn't have seen him again if he hadn't been looking for a place to live last September.

She'd accused him of being a bad friend; he'd accused her of having inane expectations. That, essentially, was the basis of every argument she and Sam had ever had. And they'd been having that argument for months now.

Elizabeth wrapped her hands around the hot mug and sighed. "I'm not an idiot, Jess. I saw a different side to Sam this past week. The side that I've always known was there, lurking under that I-don't-care-about-anything surface."

Jessica regarded Elizabeth. "You're the smartest person I know. If you can give me one example of Sam acting like a decent human being, I'll believe you."

Elizabeth smiled. "He bought me a present right after the Finn fiasco. A blank journal book with a fuzzy red cover and a cute Bugs Bunny pencil. He put a little note on the journal that said: *Thought you could use this*. Don't you think that was amazingly sweet?"

Jessica pursed her lips. "*Surprising* is what it is. So you and Sam are bosom buddies now?"

Elizabeth blushed and couldn't help the little smile that tugged at her lips.

Jessica's blue-green eyes blazed. "Something happened, didn't it!"

"Okay, okay. The other night, Wednesday to be

exact, I went down to his room to thank him for the journal, and I reached up to give him a little kiss on the cheek, but, um . . ." Elizabeth paused as the memory washed over her. She could still feel the imprint of his lips. . . . "He sort of moved his head to the side, and our lips kind of met, and, well—"

Jessica stared at her, her mouth hanging wide open.

"It was pretty intense," Elizabeth continued, "and I think it took both of us by surprise."

Jessica raised a blond eyebrow. "Ah, *now* it makes sense. Now I know why Sam's pulled his disappearing act."

Elizabeth stared down at the table.

Jessica reached across to lightly touch Elizabeth's hand. "Look, I'm not trying to be Ms. Negative here. But Sam has proved himself unable to commit to anything: studying, paying his share of the rent and bills, buying groceries, cleaning up, not to mention *relationships.*" She studied Elizabeth for a moment. "I saw him in his room Friday night—he was packing up some stuff. I told him you were worried about him, and he made some typical Sam comment about everyone being on his case all the time. He's a jerk, Liz. He's a total slacker."

"There's something good in him," Elizabeth

6

insisted. "Something very good. He acts like a jerk, yes, but it's like a cover. When I needed someone, he was there. That's all I know. And I know it sounds stupid to make a big deal about one kiss, but it was a big deal. That's why Sam's avoiding me. Because it meant something to him too."

Jessica eyed Elizabeth. "Just promise me you'll be careful, okay? You just got your heart stomped on by that jerk Finn, and I don't want you to get hurt again." Jessica looked down at her watch and jumped up. "I have to meet Jason for our running date in five minutes and don't want to be a second late. We'll talk later, okay?"

Jason? Elizabeth thought distractedly as Jessica hurried out of the kitchen. *Uh-oh.* That was the guy their housemate Neil Martin was crazy about.

She hoped Jessica knew what she was doing.

I hope you know what you're *doing,* she berated herself. *You're pining for a guy who can't deal with a kiss. Do you really think he's gonna be able to handle a relationship?*

There was only one way to find out what was going on in the unreadable mind of Sam Burgess. Elizabeth had to find him.

"I'm craving an oat-bran muffin and a cup of green tea."

Jessica glanced at Jason Wells; she hoped he

7

was kidding. Oat-bran muffin? Green tea? Ugh!

Jason was a health nut. They had already run three miles and stretched for twenty minutes, and it wasn't even ten o'clock in the morning. Every one of her muscles was screaming in pain.

"Sounds great!" she lied, twisting her body into a lunge stretch on the grass. She didn't want Jason to think she wasn't fit or flexible. The guy was hardly sweating, and he was smiling through his stretches.

Jason aimed that amazing smile of his at her, and he shot up from his own spot on the grass. "Let's jog over to Yum-Yum's."

He reached out his hand and pulled her up. His hand lingered in hers for that obvious few seconds before he pulled it away.

Aha! Jessica thought. *Jason* isn't *gay! I'm right! He's straight.* Neil Martin, her best friend and housemate, was sure that Jason was homosexual. But Jessica was ninety-nine percent positive that Jason was as straight as she was.

Jessica had been attracted to Jason from the moment she'd met him at a party about a week ago. Problem was, Neil had been attracted to Jason from the moment *he'd* met him in his political-science class. Neil was the one who'd invited Jason to the party in the first place. The very party at which Jason had flirted with Jessica. And at which

Neil insisted Jason had flirted with *him*.

But if there was one thing Jessica Wakefield knew, it was when a guy was flirting with her.

She was here with Jason only to collect proof that he wasn't gay. Then Neil would give up without making a fool of himself by coming on to a straight guy. And Jessica would give up Jason too—because she'd never go after a guy a friend liked. That wasn't cool.

But I like him so much! Jessica whined to herself. *And if he's straight, Neil couldn't really blame me, could he?*

If Jason is straight, why didn't he kiss you on your date last week? she asked herself. *But if he's gay, why didn't he make a move on Neil during their study date?*

Maybe he isn't sure if Neil is gay, she thought. *Yeah, right. Everyone knows Neil is gay. The guy outed himself during his run for student-body president.*

"Ready?" Jason asked.

"Ready," she replied, and they took off at a slow jog. "So, you and Neil got together last night?"

"Yeah, to study for econ." Jason ran his hand through his silky brown hair. "We've got a big exam on Tuesday."

They had run only half a block, but already Jessica was panting. "Wow, studying on a Saturday night—that's pretty serious. I hope you guys didn't study *all* night."

"Actually, we pretty much did," Jason answered. "Econ's pretty intense."

Jessica felt almost triumphant. "So you guys didn't fool around at all?"

"Fool around?" Jason's face was slightly flushed as he turned to look at Jessica. "What do you mean?"

Jessica swallowed. Maybe her choice of words had hit a little too close to home? "You know, fool around. Like, goof off. Watch TV, listen to music, play, um, Twister or something?"

Jason laughed. "Um, no. We just studied."

Jessica suddenly felt self-conscious about her line of questioning. "You and Neil are the only two people I know—well, besides my sister and her friend Nina—who'd spend a Saturday night studying."

"I don't mind," Jason replied. "I really like economics. It's my major, so my studying on a Saturday night is probably like you spending a Saturday night at an art gallery."

Reasonable point, Jessica thought. And interesting that he remembered she was an art-history major. He liked her, that was why!

He wasn't gay.

Right?

Nina Harper woke to the gentle shaking of her shoulder. Momentarily startled, she pulled her arm away, snuggling it underneath her chest, and burrowed her cheek into her warm pillow.

Correction: Josh's warm pillow.

"Nina, are you awake?" he asked.

"Mmmm, hi," she said, letting her eyes stay closed. She felt so good! A little electric thrill coursed through her veins. Here she was, waking up with Josh for the first time.

He reached over her to turn on the radio. The sound of Britney Spears filled the room.

Nina opened her eyes, squinting against the sunlight streaming through the dust motes swirling in the air of his dorm room. She turned around to face him and looked into his blue eyes. *Oh,* she thought, *he is too cute.*

Closing her eyes again, Nina snuggled her face into Josh's warm chest. She could hang out in bed with him all day!

"Uh, so . . . I've got a lot of stuff to do . . . ," Josh said stiffly.

He reached over her again to change the radio station. Suddenly the raw-metal chords of Korn blasted through the room. Nina put her hand over her eyes to shield them against the too bright sunshine. Josh got out of bed and walked over to his desk. He turned on his computer.

Okay, so that wasn't very romantic, Nina thought. *But he's serious about his schoolwork. That's the major reason you like him, don't forget. Because he's not a musician in love with himself the way Xavier was.* Nina blinked against the memory of Xavier; she refused to think about him or how much he'd hurt her.

Josh was nothing like Xavier. He was a serious engineering major. And she was a serious physics major. They made a logical pair. *We're such a couple of geeks!* she thought happily as Josh's modem made its nasty blaring sound as it connected to the network.

Nina sat up and smiled at Josh's back; he was staring intently at the monitor. "What's that?" she asked.

"An e-mail from my cousin Paul," he said distract-edly.

Nina stared at his back for a moment. It was hard to feel ignored in a room this small, but that was the vibe she was starting to pick up. She crossed her arms over her chest and looked under the bed for her shoes. Her brand-new mules were covered with dust bunnies. She glanced down at the condition of her clothes, which she'd slept in. Her tight black shirt had lint all over it, and her ice blue capri pants were badly wrinkled. Nina winced. She'd paid a fortune for those pants!

Nina took a deep breath. "So, um, I thought

we'd grab some breakfast at Yum-Yum's or the Red Lion, then hit the library and study together. Sound good?"

He clicked away at the keyboard. "I told some friends I'd meet them for breakfast, so . . ."

"Oh, okay," Nina said. "That sounds nice."

Josh still didn't take his eyes off the monitor. "I have to be there in like fifteen minutes, so, um, you know, I'd better get going."

Nina paused. *I*, not *we*. He wasn't even going to invite her to come with him to breakfast. He just wanted her to get out of his room.

Or maybe Nina was just being insecure.

As he shut off his computer, Nina put on her shoes, then rummaged through her purse for her compact. She studied herself in the tiny mirror. Her wild, shoulder-length curls were a bit flattened, but overall she looked okay.

As she dropped the compact in her bag, she realized that Josh was waiting for her to leave.

Humiliating. Just like catching Xavier making out with another girl when he was supposed to be into her. *Was* Josh another Xavier? Suddenly turning off because she wouldn't have sex with him?

Am I being a prude? she wondered. She'd gone out with Josh only once. Was she supposed to have sex with him on the first date?

Nina stood up slowly. "Well, Josh," she said,

forcing a smile as she stepped to the door. "I'll be in the library most of the day."

He nodded. "Uh, yeah, um, maybe I'll see you there later."

Yeah, sure, she thought. Josh awkwardly moved as if to hug her, but then sat back down at his desk. "Bye," she said, then slipped out.

Nina felt eyes on her as she hurried down the hall of his dorm. His floor mates had seen her come out of his room. Embarrassing. It was like everyone knowing she'd just had sex, even though she hadn't!

She squinted again against the bright sunlight as she exited the dorm and headed toward her own. She was aware of how inappropriate her outfit was for a Sunday morning. Now *everyone* would know she was returning from an all-night date.

Sam Burgess woke to the chest-thumping bass line and earsplitting drum track that accompanied the hip-hop song blasting from the stereo. Through two tired eyes he glared across the room at his friend Bugsy, sleeping peacefully in his own bed.

There was no way he could camp out on Bugsy's floor in his hot, sweaty sleeping bag for another night. Bugs was a cool guy, but he

14

couldn't fall asleep without music blasting in his ears, and he smoked constantly, which made Sam sick to his stomach. He'd rather sleep in his car than spend another night gasping for air with his hands clamped over his ears.

Sam slowly emerged from his sweaty cocoon. He stood up and stretched, then pulled on his black T-shirt and let it hang over the rim of his faded Levi's.

He reached for the stereo and turned down the volume a few levels.

"What?" Bugsy jerked up out of bed. "Why'd you turn that down, dude? You're messing up my REM sleep!"

"Bugs," Sam answered. "It's almost two P.M. What you need to do is get your lazy butt out of bed."

Bugsy closed his eyes and turned over. "Okay, *Mom*."

Sam snorted. "If I were your mom, I'd tell you to clean your room. Seriously, Bugs, this place is disgusting. I just stepped on a tortilla chip, man."

"Hey, dude, I'm doing you a favor by letting you stay here," Bugsy said as he sat up and yawned. "Don't forget you've got Girl Who Wants to Talk at your place."

Sam grimaced and ran a hand through his

sandy brown hair. "I know," he said. "Believe me, I know."

"Look, dude, it's not like she can force you to have some big relationship talk. Just refuse to."

"But you do not understand," Sam answered in a lame sinister-German accent. "Shee has vays of making mee talk."

Bugsy laughed. "But what are you gonna do? I mean, you gotta go home sometime, right?"

"Do I?" Sam asked.

"Well, you obviously don't want to spend another night on my floor." Bugsy sniffed, trying to sound insulted. "What about Anna? I'm sure she'd let you crash at her place."

Sam wished he could stay at his good friend Anna's. "No can do, dude. Her dorky roommate won't let her have guys spend the night."

"What?" Bugsy was taken aback. "Doesn't she understand that this is the twenty-first century? Besides, you guys are just friends, right?"

Sam shrugged. "Yeah. We are. But her roommate's just really uptight. It's weird because Anna is so cool."

"Well, dude," Bugsy offered apologetically, "even if you did want to stay here another night, I'm afraid the answer is no."

"Huh?" Sam flashed him a puzzled look.

"You see, Sammy boy, ol' Bugsy's got himself a

date tonight." He smiled devilishly and rubbed his hands together. "And I think I just might get lucky."

Sam looked at him like he had to be joking. The thought of Bugsy on a date *was* a joke. "In that case, I think I better leave you here alone—to clean your room."

Chapter Two

Jessica sipped her green tea, trying not to notice that everyone else in Yum-Yum's Café had delicious-looking, unhealthy breakfast treats in front of them. What she would give to have a mocchacino and a double-fudge brownie!

Jason, sitting across from her, shifted in his over-stuffed chair, and Jessica's eyes were glued to his amazing shoulder muscles moving up and down. Could a guy be any more gorgeous, any more built? Jessica wondered, trying not to stare. She loved the way his navy blue sweater complemented his eyes. The way his jeans fit perfectly. The way one of his sneakers had come untied . . .

You're losing it, she told herself. *And he's not yours to like. You'd better not forget it.*

"So how's the muffin?" Jason asked, flashing her his killer smile. "Delicious, huh?"

Jessica smiled and took a small bite. It tasted like it was made of concrete. "It's so healthy tasting!" she said enthusiastically. Jason took another bite of his muffin and closed his eyes, savoring it as if it were a chocolate bar. All of a sudden she didn't mind drinking bitter green tea and eating a bone-dry, boring oat muffin.

Sitting in a public place with one of the best-looking guys on campus was worth a million taste-less muffins, Jessica thought as she gazed around the café. She spotted the side of a familiar head coming toward her and Jason's table. She'd know Chloe Murphy's trademark red hair anywhere.

"Hey, Chlo," Jessica called out.

But the girl didn't look up. In fact, Chloe was keeping her head to the side, as if she was trying to hide her face from the world at large.

"Chloe?" Jessica tried again. Maybe it wasn't her.

The redhead turned face forward. It was Chloe. But she didn't look very happy. The guy standing bedside her, holding a tray laden with the goodies Jessica was craving, however, did. He looked particularly happy. He looked familiar too. But Jessica couldn't remember where she'd seen him before.

What was up with Chloe? Jessica wondered. Her freshman Theta sister was usually gushing hellos at Jessica and the other Theta government officers.

Suddenly Jessica realized where she'd seen the guy with Chloe. She'd seen him talking to Chloe at the very party at which she'd met Jason.

"Oh, hey, Jessica," Chloe said stiffly. "I can't believe this place is so busy so early. I thought it would be empty this early on a Sunday morning."

"It's because they have the best oat-bran muffins on campus," Jason said. "Hi—I'm Jason Wells, by the way."

He was so cool, Jessica thought. Friendly, outgoing, polite. Perfect!

"Jason, this is Chloe Murphy. She's one of my sorority sisters and lives in Theta house. And this is her . . ." Jessica trailed off so that Chloe could introduce her friend.

Chloe seemed nervous about something, Jessica noticed. "Jessica, Jason, this is, um, Martin. Well, we'd better go find a table. Bye!"

Since the only open table was next to Jason and Jessica's, Chloe and her friend didn't get very far. *Note to self,* Jessica mentally told herself. *Call Chloe later and find out what her deal is. She's acting really weird!*

Chloe leaned close to Jessica and whispered, "Jason is so hot!"

Now that was more like the Chloe she knew and sort of loved. But Jessica didn't need anyone to remind her of how amazing-looking Jason Wells was!

The question was: Was she hot to Jason? Jessica still couldn't tell. She liked the way he looked at her. *Interested*, but not foaming at the mouth. *But is he interested?* she wondered for the millionth time.

"Hey, Jess," Chloe said, "want a piece of my double-fudge brownie?"

Jessica turned and eyed the chocolate wonder. Her mouth started watering. She felt Jason's gorgeous eyes on her. "Um, no, thanks, Chloe. I've been on a healthful-eating plan for a while now. It does look good, though."

"It is," Martin whispered, biting into his and closing his eyes as he savored the brownie. Somehow sweet but nerdy-looking Martin didn't have the same effect on Jessica that Jason had when he'd done the very same thing! "It's amazing. Good choice, Chloe!" He slung his arm around Chloe's shoulders with a big smile on his face.

Chloe's face turned red, and she quickly moved so that Martin would have to drop his arm. Martin seemed oblivious to the fact that Chloe didn't want his arm around her. He wiggled closer to Chloe and put his arm around her again.

"We'd better go, Martin," Chloe said, shooting up and stuffing their coffees and brownies into a paper bag. Her movement made Martin's arm fall again. "We can sneak our breakfast into the library."

As Chloe rushed to leave, Martin waved good-bye and trailed after her like a puppy.

Jessica let out a little laugh. "I think Chloe's embarrassed to be seen with Martin in public! Did you see the way she kept trying to keep his arm off her? I'm glad to see her with a regular guy who'll like her back for once. She tends to go for trophy guys who ignore her, like SVU's quarterback and my housemate Sam. But I get the feeling Martin isn't BMOC enough for Chloe."

Jason smiled. "Poor guy. He clearly has a major crush on the girl. The old arm-around-the-shoulders move is a dead giveaway."

And with a sly smile, Jason put his own arm around Jessica.

Neil Martin sat cross-legged on his bed and stared at the phone for five minutes before he could pick it up. He couldn't seem to work up the nerve to dial Jason's entire phone number. Six digits was about as far as he ever got. In this day of *69 and caller ID, Neil knew that once you dialed that seventh digit, there was no turning back.

What was he so worried about? It wasn't like he had never called Jason on the phone before. And Jason had called him back plenty of times.

Called him *back*. That was the key. Jason never seemed to call Neil unless he was calling him back.

never *initiated* contact. Neil was constantly putting the ball in Jason's court. And while he was always game to volley, Jason never went in for the slam.

"Just call him," Neil said out loud to himself. He looked out the window at the setting sun. Neil had been planning to ask Jason to grab some dinner, and if he didn't call soon, he could forget it.

What's the big deal? he asked himself. *Just call.*

Neil knew what the big deal was: Jessica's claims that Jason wasn't gay. But Neil was ninety-nine-point-nine percent sure that Jason Wells was as gay as Neil was. No. There was another big deal. One that was making Neil really nervous.

Jason is the first guy you've liked since you left Stanford last summer, he reminded himself. *You're finally ready to have a relationship. This is a major step for you. But you can't take that step unless you get some guts and make the call!*

Neil finally picked up the phone and started dialing. All seven digits. As he listened to the phone ring, he realized that he had no idea what he was going to say when Jason answered.

"Hello?"

Neil coughed. "Hey, Jason, it's Neil."

"Hey, Neil," Jason said. "What's up?"

"Um, well, I thought maybe you'd want to

24

grab a burger at the Red Lion or something. I'm starving."

"Sounds good, but I can't," Jason replied. "I think I pulled a muscle in my leg during my run earlier. It's funny—I'm a major runner, and I pull a muscle. Your housemate Jessica fesses up that she rarely runs, and she felt great after our three-mile morning."

Neil felt the hairs on the back of his neck stand up. Jason went running with Jessica this morning? Why hadn't she mentioned it when he saw her earlier this afternoon? *Because she's going after him herself,* he thought bitterly. *That's why. Your best friend is going after the first guy you've allowed yourself to like since transferring to SVU.*

"Well, um, Jason, I guess I'll just see you in econ, then."

"Thanks for the invite, though, Neil. Maybe some other time."

Neil hung up, feeling weird and stupid about the whole thing. He wished he hadn't called. *Maybe some other time . . .*

Was that a blow off? Or did Jason really pull a muscle? *Argh!* Neil thought. He felt so confused. Was Jason gay or not?

And *was* Jessica going after the guy Neil liked? She was his best friend. No way would she really do something like that to him. She knew about everything he'd gone through at Stanford. That he'd never been ready to date until now.

No, Jessica would never betray him, Neil thought.

Would she?

Sam strained his eyes, trying to see through the rain-splashed windshield of his beat-up old car. He didn't know what was more annoying: the incessant whine of the worn-out wipers or the fact that it was impossible to see more than about twenty feet in front of the car. To top it all off, the tape deck was broken and the only radio station coming in clearly was the one that played "all love songs, all the time."

He felt like such a cheeseball: Every time a new song came on, he caught himself thinking about Elizabeth. Then of course he would think of going home and facing her. And then he'd try to think of someone who might possibly put him up for the next couple of days.

That's all he needed: just a couple of days to get his head together. Then he'd be able to face Elizabeth.

Or would he?

What was his problem? What was so difficult all of a sudden? Why did one little kiss have to change everything so drastically? He had been driving around for hours. Around and around, just like the thoughts inside his head.

26

Sam wished he had somewhere to go. Somewhere he wouldn't run into anyone he knew. Somewhere he could think. Somewhere where Elizabeth's inevitable questions would stop ringing in his ears.

Where have you been? Why have you been avoiding me? Where do we go from here?

Sam thought again about his options. Bugsy, no. Even if he had offered his floor again, Sam knew he couldn't spend another night in that stinky sweatbox.

He couldn't stay at Floyd's either. The last time Floyd had offered Sam a place to crash, he had kicked him out at the last minute to make room for some goth chick who didn't even end up spending the night. Sam had found himself in the dorm's TV lounge, trying in vain to sleep while a bunch of nerds stayed up watching a *Star Trek* marathon. He wasn't going to take that chance again.

And he couldn't stay with his good buddy Anna because of her uptight roommate.

At this point Sam was ready to check into a cheap motel. There was simply nowhere else to go. If the weather was nice, he would have slept on the beach. But it wasn't.

Sam made his way through the rain-drenched night to Commercial Boulevard, where all the affordable motels were clustered. He was willing to stay just about anywhere. Anywhere besides home. But after passing the fourth vacancy sign with the neon No lit up in red, Sam realized he was out of luck.

The big sign outside the Sweet Valley Motor Lodge read: Welcome, Cal Central Wildcats. Go, SVU! right above the bright red No Vacancy.

Sam finally remembered that it was the night of the huge football game between SVU and their archrivals, CCU. Without having to drive any farther, Sam knew that every motel on the strip would be filled.

Again he thought about going home. And again he insisted to himself he couldn't. Sam knew he was being a total chump, but so be it. He wasn't going to go back to face Elizabeth until he actually had something to say. If only he could stay at Anna's or at least see her. He was sure Anna could give him some good advice on how to deal with the situation.

As his thoughts drifted back and forth between various couches and floors, reclining bucket seats, tacky motel bedspreads, and visions of Elizabeth standing with her arms crossed in the doorway to his bedroom, Sam realized that the strip of motels on Commercial had ended a long time ago. Instead of big neon lights mocking him with their promise of shelter and warmth for visiting football fans, there were hardly any lights left at all.

Dark, grassy hills extended as far as his limited vision in either direction, soaking up the pouring rain and absorbing the dark of the night. He knew immediately where he was: Country Club Road.

As Sam cruised past the mansions of Sweet Valley, his smile faded. His stomach tightened. He knew what was coming up.

No sooner had he thought it than it appeared before him: the glorious facade of the Sweet Valley Resort Hotel. It jumped out of the night in all its splendor, offering not just warmth and shelter, but absolute luxury. Luxury for free.

Because Sam Burgess's very wealthy parents *owned* the hotel.

And the thought of staying there, even for one night, made him sick to his stomach.

Her arms full of her heavy physics textbooks, Nina kicked shut her dorm-room door with her foot. She dropped her books and binders on her desk, then checked her answering machine.

No message from Josh.

Great. She'd spent all day in the library, trying to concentrate but not succeeding. She'd been unable to get him and this morning out of her mind. But she'd forced herself to stay in that hard-backed, uncomfortable library chair, her textbooks in front

29

of her, because she'd been sure there would be a treat waiting for her when she returned to her room. A treat in the form of an apologetic message from Josh.

Ha.

She hadn't given him what he wanted—sex—so he wasn't giving her what she wanted: a relationship. Or at least a start of one!

If he wasn't going to take it as slowly as she wanted, then he was just going to have to do without her. And she without him. But that was the hard part because she really liked him.

Maybe it was just the awkwardness of a relationship starting out. Nina didn't really know how strongly she felt about Josh, so maybe he didn't know about her either. And sometimes it was hard to concentrate on another person's feelings when you didn't know what you thought about him. Or her. Maybe he hadn't even meant to be cold like that—maybe he'd just wanted a little space to think things over.

Why did the whole thing have to be so difficult? she wondered, collapsing onto her bed. If only relationships were like studying. In studying, everything was so clear! When you had the right answer, you *knew* it was right. Well, physics would always be there for her.

The telephone's bright, electronic ring jarred her senses. Nina lunged for it.

"Hello?"

"Hi, Nina. It's Josh."

Well, well, she thought. "Hey."

"So, I looked for you in the library this afternoon," he said. "I didn't see you."

Then you didn't look very hard, she felt like yelling into the phone.

"I thought I'd come visit you if you're into it," he half said, half asked.

Into what? she wondered. *Into fooling around? Into you trying to convince me to have sex with you? Or into visiting me because you like me and want to see me?*

"Look, Josh, I'd like to, but tonight's not good for me. I have to finish reading *The Sun Also Rises* for English, and then I have to write a paper, so . . ."

"So how about later tonight?" he suggested.

When? Midnight? Oh, that's really romantic. "Why don't you find me in the library tomorrow around three, and maybe we can go for a late lunch or something?"

"Um, okay," he said hesitantly. "I'll find you in the library. See you tomorrow."

Yeah, Nina thought as she hung up. *Right. Like I'll ever see you again. You didn't get any last night, and I've just turned you down for tonight, so forget about a date tomorrow that might not lead to what you want.*

How was Nina supposed to concentrate on Hemingway now?

Chapter
Three

"Good evening, Mr. Burgess. How can we be of service to you this evening?"

The stiff, bespectacled, birdlike attendant behind the vast marble counter greeted Sam as if he were dressed in an Armani suit and holding an attaché case.

Sam couldn't believe he was even allowed in the front door, let alone that he was being addressed by name. He wondered if his picture was posted somewhere behind the desk. Perhaps with a warning to treat him with the utmost caution.

Warning. Estranged son of Sweet Valley Resort Hotel owners. Irresponsible slacker who's never had a job. Chose to attend Orange County College just to irritate parents. Thinks he knows it all. If possible, lull him into a false sense of luxury and then detain him until Mr. and Mrs. Burgess arrive.

The attendant didn't seem to be activating any secret alarms. In fact, he continued to treat him as if he owned the place. Which, Sam was sorry to admit, he actually did. For tax purposes the ownership of the resort was in *his* name rather than his father's. So in effect he could do anything he wanted here. Only Sam didn't want to do anything.

It's just for one night, he insisted to himself. *And I won't even order room service.*

"I trust the owner's suite will be acceptable for you, Mr. Burgess?" the bird man said. "The entire hotel is booked, you'll be glad to know. Big game between SVU and its rival."

Sam realized he hadn't said a word since he approached the front desk. He just stood dripping on the floor as the clerk peered down his nose at him with restrained respect.

The pomp and circumstance of the lobby, not to mention the sensation of being treated as if he belonged here, made Sam uncomfortable. And he knew the lavish owner's suite would be even more overwhelming. Especially since it contained so many of his family's personal effects, from the silver-framed family photos symmetrically arrayed on the mantel to the oil paintings of his father and his father's father in the large sitting room.

"I'll take the owner's suite if that's all that's available."

"Very well, then." Spectacles handed Sam the key card and managed a lifeless half smile. "Will you be needing any help with your luggage, Mr. Burgess?"

"Nah, I think I can manage," Sam answered with a smirk.

The ridiculousness of the scene was almost over-whelming. Parking his crummy car in the VIP spot. Showing up at the desk in his wet, dirty clothes and now being given the royal treatment.

Sam squished down the plush-carpeted corridor of the Sweet Valley Resort Hotel in his soggy sneakers.

When he reached the ornate door marked Owner's Suite, Sam finally felt relieved. At last he had some privacy. And soon a shower.

He entered the room and stripped off his clothes, then turned on the shower and stepped underneath the hard, hot spray. The way the water pelted his back tempted Sam to order a massage in the morn-ing. As long as he was taking advantage of his birthright, he might as well take it all the way, right?

But no sooner had the thought crossed his mind than the deep, cleansing shower made him feel slightly dingy. Not dirty, but tarnished. *What good are personal convictions if you're just going to violate them for the sake of avoiding a girl?*

Sam reached down and turned off the water, hoping the clockwise motion of the shower knob would also work to turn off his thoughts about Elizabeth.

As he emerged from the bathroom wrapped in a fluffy white towel, Sam eyed his dirty, wet pile of clothes with disgust. There was no way he was going to put those on now. No way.

Sam spotted the phone, resting on its special little baroque table. He called housekeeping and arranged for his laundry to be picked up and delivered back to him in an hour. Then he dialed his friend Anna's number.

"Hello?"

"Anna, it's Sam. I've got an offer you can't refuse. How about spending the night in the lap of luxury? And don't worry. I'm not trying to seduce you."

She laughed. "You're not, huh? Then what's in it for me?"

He chuckled. "Like I said, a night in the lap of luxury."

"Ah," she said. "Well, then, what's in it for you?"

Sam sighed. "Um, well, to tell you the truth, I could use some advice. I'm at the Sweet Valley Resort Hotel."

"The Sweet Valley Resort Hotel?" she repeated incredulously. "You must be joking."

"It's no joke. Just come on over and tell the guy at the desk you're here to see me, and he'll show you to my room."

"*Your* room? You *must* be joking."

"Really, Anna, I'm not. Just come on over, and I'll explain everything."

"Okay. See you soon."

Sam hung up the phone and breathed a sigh of relief. If he was going to be stuck in this strange, familiar universe for the night, at least he'd have a friend to talk to.

Elizabeth pulled open the door to Snack Attack and stepped inside. The small café on OCC's campus was packed with students munching away on nachos, sandwiches, and fries, textbooks open before them on little round tables.

But Sam Burgess wasn't among them.

Elizabeth sighed and dropped down on a chair. There were couples all around her. Couples feeding each other nachos. Couples giggling. Couples with their legs intertwined underneath the table as they studied together.

And couples coming in, going out. Couples together.

Yet here Elizabeth sat, totally alone among all these people. Suddenly she shivered, feeling exposed, as if everyone was looking at her and knew what she was doing. *That girl's hunting everywhere for some guy who couldn't even handle a kiss! What a naive idiot she must be! Why is she chasing him? He*

37

should be on his knees, begging her to forgive him, begging her to give him another chance!

Elizabeth leaned back in her chair. She'd say all that and then some if someone had asked her advice for the very situation she was in. Especially since Sam was the guy in question.

But no one had been in his car with them the night he'd picked her up from that bar outside Finn's apartment, the bar where she'd gone to make a phone call after Finn had thrown her out. She'd prayed Jessica would be home as she dialed. All she'd wanted that night was for her sister to come get her so she could cry her eyes out on Jessica's shoulder. But Jessica hadn't been home. And Sam had come to get her.

Sam Burgess. He'd wordlessly helped her into his car, then drove and drove until he parked at a secluded overlook, where she sobbed out the whole horrible story and then sobbed and sobbed against his chest. And all the while he hadn't said *I told you so*. He hadn't said much at all. He'd just held her, stroked her hair, and told her everything would be all right.

And everything had been all right. Until now.

Sam Burgess was worth looking for, whether anyone else thought so or not.

Her resolve strengthened, Elizabeth stood up and headed out of the shop. She looked to the left and to the right, as if Sam would mysteriously appear on the block.

She had no idea where to check next. She'd already combed the OCC student center, every campus bar, the arcade, and the mall and then rechecked campus hot spots where students seemed to congregate. There had been no sign of him.

Where could he be? she wondered as she pulled open the door to her Jeep and climbed inside. She had no idea where his two idiotic friends Bugsy and Floyd lived, so she couldn't try to track them down. She'd just have to go home. And wait.

He'd come home eventually, wouldn't he?

"Sam, what on earth are you doing here?" Anna asked him the minute he opened the door. "I mean, how can you afford all of this?"

Sam mentally kicked himself. He'd been so busy thinking about his nonrelationship with Elizabeth that he hadn't considered what he was going to tell Anna about his ritzy room. "I know the owner."

"Oh, yeah?" Anna looked dubiously at Sam.

"Yeah." Sam patted her on the shoulder. "For real. Everything's taken care of. And don't worry—it's all legal. Now, do you want to get room service or what?"

"No, you go ahead. I'll just have coffee." Anna continued to scan the room. "Sam, really, what's the deal with this place? What are you doing here?"

"Like I said, I know the owners."

"All right, Mr. Mysterious." Anna relented. "So why aren't you at your own house? It's not like you live that far away."

Sam snorted. "If you had a choice, which would you choose?"

"Well, you've got a point there," Anna answered uncertainly.

"Seriously, though, I just thought it'd be fun to get away for a little while, you know?"

"Oh, yeah, is that why I haven't been able to reach you on the phone?" Anna asked in a concerned voice. "You know, I talked to Elizabeth today, and she sounded really worried."

Now it was Sam who sounded concerned. "You talked to Elizabeth? Why?"

"I was calling for you," Anna said, eyebrow raised. "Aha. So this is about Elizabeth again. You are into her."

Sam sighed and put his head in his hands.

"I see we've got a lot to talk about," Anna said. "Last I knew about you and Lizzie was that you saved her from the evil virgin killer, Finn Something, right? So then what happened?"

"Do we have to talk about this right now?" Sam pleaded as he raised his head and stared at the ceiling.

"Why not? Isn't that the reason you called me out here?"

Sam let out a deep breath. "I just wanted someone to talk to. And not necessarily about Elizabeth."

"All right." Anna sighed. "Suit yourself. But the sooner you tell me what's going on, the sooner I can help you deal with it. And the sooner you'll be living in your own house. Not that this place isn't nice," she added with a sly smile.

Why did Anna always have to be right? Sam wondered as she leaned back in the very comfy upholstered chair. Anna was one of his best friends and the only female friend he had. She challenged him, the way he expected his friends to do. But he wasn't attracted to her, nor she to him, and so their friendship was perfect for both of them. They always told each other the truth, and they were able to get the perspective of the opposite sex.

Sam smiled at her. "I know, I know."

"So what happened?" Anna repeated. "Do you want to talk about this or not?"

"Yeah, I guess so," Sam reluctantly consented. "But it's, like, kind of a long story."

"Hey, I've got all night," Anna answered, smiling. "And as long as we're staying at the fashionable Sweet Valley Resort Hotel, I might as well make the most of it. So tell me everything."

Sam took a deep breath. "Okay, so you know the whole deal with Finn, right?"

"Right."

"Well," Sam continued, "after all of that blew over, I don't know, it's like Elizabeth really changed or something. At first she was just, like, really depressed, and she hardly ever came out of her room."

"Uh-huh, that's understandable."

"But whenever I did see her," Sam continued, "she was acting sort of different toward me. Nicer somehow. Softer . . ." Sam paused, thinking back on those days between Finn and the Kiss.

"Well," Anna interjected, "after the whole Finn fiasco, she must have realized that you weren't such a jerk after all."

Sam shot her a look.

"Okay, I'm just kidding!" Anna said. "Go on."

"So, I don't know. She was much nicer to me, but I could tell that she just wasn't doing well. You know, in general."

"Uh-huh."

"So I gave her this stupid little present—some dumb Bugs Bunny pencil and a fuzzy-covered journal—and I wrote her a little note telling her that I thought she could use it, you know, to write down her feelings." Sam spoke rapidly, like he couldn't wait to get the words out of his mouth. Then he looked up at Anna for her response.

She looked like she was about to cry.

"Oh, Sam, you are so sweet," she cooed. "I swear, if I wasn't involved with Leonardo DiCaprio right now—"

"Oh, shut up," Sam snapped at her playfully.

"Seriously, Sam." Anna looked up at him with a perfectly straight face. "You are such a sweetheart. I mean, what girl wouldn't adore you?"

"Thanks, Anna. Thanks a lot. But I need advice, not an ego boost, okay?"

Anna smiled and nodded.

"Okay, so I gave her the stupid little present." Sam took another deep breath. Even though Anna was one of his best friends, he still felt slightly uncomfortable telling another girl the details of his love life. "So, anyway, she came down to my room that night—I guess to thank me—and, well, she leaned in to give me this little kiss on the cheek. And I guess I didn't quite get what was going on, so I turned my head. And then we started to kiss. And it got, like, kind of intense. But really it only lasted for a couple of seconds. And then Elizabeth got all flustered and she all but ran away—back to her room—and I, like, didn't know what to do."

"So you took off with your tail between your legs and never looked back," Anna finished the story for him.

"Yeah," Sam agreed, "that's basically it."

Anna clucked. "Sam, Sam, Sam. What are we going to do with you, huh? You show these flashes of extreme sweetness, and then it's like you remember you're a *guy* or something."

"Anna, I *am* a guy," Sam sarcastically reminded her.

"I know." Anna sighed again. "That's the problem."

"So what do I do now?" Sam whined.

"Well, I think by now you probably know what I'm going to tell you, Sam," Anna began.

Sam had to admit that Anna's ability to get all parental on him was another of the things he really liked about her. Not that she was a nag or a goody-goody. Usually she was just into having fun, goofing around, hanging out, or whatever. But when he really needed her, she was able to come through for him like his mom or dad—or even his older brother—never could. And he did have a pretty good idea what she was going to tell him.

"What, just tell her the truth about how I really feel?" Sam guessed.

"Well, yeah. But first you've got to figure out for yourself what that really is. I think I have a feeling what your avoidance behavior is all about, though."

"Avoidance behavior? Anna, have you ever thought of becoming a psychotherapist?"

"But then I'd have to charge you for these little sessions," she teased. "So, tell me, Sam: How *do* you really feel about Elizabeth?"

This was the inevitable question that Sam had been fearing. "Well, I guess I really like her, but . . ." Sam's answer trailed off.

"But what?" Anna prompted him.

Sam stared at his bare feet. "I don't know."

"Sam, tell me the major reason you really like me as a friend," Anna said.

"Because you totally challenge me, like you're doing now," he said, shooting her a dirty look. "Suddenly I don't like it after all."

"Aha!" she said. "Now, tell me why we're not involved in a relationship."

What was she getting at? Sam wondered. Anna was really smart, so she was definitely trying to lead him somewhere. He didn't get it, but he'd play along. He might as well.

"We're not in a relationship because we don't have any physical chemistry. We've never been attracted to each other."

"Aha!" Anna said again, this time with a snap of her fingers.

"And are you attracted to Elizabeth?" she asked.

Sam laughed. "Beyond attracted. I dream about the girl."

"Does she challenge you like I do?"

"Anna, you know she does. That's why she and I fight all the time. She's always—"

Suddenly Sam understood what Anna was trying to make him realize.

"So," he said, "I'm avoiding her because it's too much to deal with. I'm finally attracted to a girl I could be real friends with. A girl who challenges me, holds me accountable, expects stuff from me. And I can't deal. Because it's too real."

"Bingo," Anna said, leaning back against the plush chair. "Sam, remember something. Elizabeth is obviously crazy about you. If she wants you bad enough, she'll back off a little, give you the space you idiotically need."

"Maybe *that* is exactly what I'm afraid of," Sam explained.

"What?"

"That she'll be too sweet and nice and giving, and I'll feel pressured all the time. Oh, man, I don't know. I don't even know what I'm saying."

"Does the fact that she's a virgin have anything to do with it?" Anna asked. "You're afraid to be her 'first.' Too much responsibility?"

Sam almost groaned aloud. Why did Anna have to understand him so well? "It's not just that I'm afraid to be her 'first.' " As he spoke, Sam was trying to understand his feelings well enough to put them into words. "It's what she's gonna expect, I think. Everything I say, do, think—she'll analyze it the way she always does, ask me tons of questions, judge everything I say and do. Expect this and that. Man, it's just too much. And all the while she'll know me too well, like you do. She'll know when I'm lying or trying to sneak out of something."

"Sam," Anna said, leaning forward with a serious look on her face. "It sounds like you're in love with this girl."

"What?" Sam shrieked.

Anna smiled. "You heard me. Look, buddy, I think you'd better suck up your fears and talk to Elizabeth. You don't have to conquer everything that scares you to death all at once. Just talk to her. Tell her the *truth*."

"That you think I'm in love with her?"

Anna shook her head. "That you're scared and have no idea what you want except for the fact that you want her."

Sam stared at Anna. "I'm allowed to say that?"

"*Hello?* Isn't that the truth? The only truth?"

Sam nodded.

Anna smiled and stood up from the edge of the chair. "All right. Now, how about that room service? Figuring out your life has made me hungry after all."

Chapter Four

Elizabeth rolled out of bed and slipped into her fuzzy pink slippers all in one motion.

Some mornings she never wanted to leave the cozy sanctuary beneath the fluffy white comforter of her queen-size bed. But this morning was different. The night before had been bad enough.

She had spent the bulk of it trying to stay awake, listening for Sam to come home. The last time she remembered looking at her alarm clock was 2:45 A.M.

So she hadn't exactly gotten her full eight hours. But now that it was morning, she had only one thing on her mind: finding out if Sam had returned while she was asleep. If he hadn't, she was going to go looking for him again. That was the last promise she'd made to herself before falling asleep.

She hastily pulled her bathrobe around her

shoulders and rushed into the hallway, tying the robe in front on her way downstairs. She practically sprinted through the kitchen to Sam's room and was supremely relieved to see his door closed.

It had been open the night before, hadn't it? The fact that it was now closed had to mean that he was in there.

He had come home at last.

But Elizabeth had to be sure. She walked softly to the door and put her ear to it, listening for any sign of life. Nothing. Her heart raced as she tapped lightly on the door. As she waited for an answer, Elizabeth realized that she had no idea what she would say if he happened to be in there.

There was no response, so she tapped again, this time with a bit more force. She strained to listen but heard nothing from inside. She had no choice—she had to open the door and see if he was in there. If he was, she prayed he was alone.

As quietly as possible, she slowly turned the doorknob. If he did happen to be inside, there was no point in waking him. For now she'd be happy just to know he was there. Just to know he was alive.

He'd have plenty of time to explain himself later.

Elizabeth pushed open the door just enough to see and peered inside.

Her heart sank at the sight of his unmade bed,

each wrinkle of his sheets in exactly the same position as it had been the day before.

She couldn't believe it. That was four nights in a row he hadn't come home. And there was no sign he had been in the house during the daytime either. And not even one phone call to her and the other housemates to let them know that he was all right.

Something had to be wrong. Elizabeth thought about who she could call to check on him. She had no idea where his parents even lived. And judging by the way Sam talked about them, she was sure they would have no more clues to his whereabouts than she did. There was that Anna girl who'd called for Sam yesterday. But she clearly didn't know where Sam was either. And the last person Elizabeth wanted to call was one of Sam's sexual conquests.

Elizabeth was desperate. Why couldn't he just call? Just a simple phone call, just to let her know that he was all right. Was that too much to ask?

Then, as if in answer to her prayers, the phone rang. It was actually ringing. And at this hour of the day on Monday, who could it possibly be *but* Sam? She practically lunged for the phone.

"Hello?" Elizabeth failed to hide the desperation in her voice.

"Elizabeth?" It wasn't Sam.

"Oh, hey, Nina."

"Jeez, don't sound *too* happy to hear from me. Where have *you* been? I tried to call you a bunch of times last night."

"Um, nowhere . . . Here . . . I don't know." Elizabeth didn't have the patience for small talk. She had too much on her mind.

"Well, that's pretty vague," Nina snapped. "So, what's been happening?"

"Oh, not much," Elizabeth answered distractedly. "You know, school and stuff."

"School and stuff?" Nina asked crossly. "Um, Elizabeth, do you even know who this is? It's Nina. Nina Harper, your best friend?"

"Yes, Nina, I know it's you." Elizabeth couldn't help sounding cross as well. "Listen, I'm kind of busy right now, to tell you the truth. . . ."

"Busy? Elizabeth, I know you don't have a class till later this morning, so—oh, wait, I'm sorry. Are you with someone?" Nina suddenly sounded embarrassed.

With someone, right, Elizabeth thought. *I'm the opposite of "with someone."*

"Who would I possibly be with, Nina?" she demanded, then realized how awful she sounded. "I'm sorry. I think I woke up on the wrong side of bed. Let's start over, okay? What's up?"

Nina's voice softened. "I just wanted to talk to you about this guy I've been seeing."

Elizabeth was surprised. "You're seeing someone? Who?"

"His name's Josh," Nina began. "I'm not really 'seeing' seeing him—we've just been fooling around and stuff."

Elizabeth drifted back to her memory of the Kiss. The smell of Sam's soap as she'd leaned close to him. The intensity of his hazel eyes boring into her own as they'd come apart, stunned by what had just happened . . .

"So, I don't know," Nina continued tentatively. "I'm just not sure what's going on. . . ."

"Mm-hmmm," Elizabeth muttered.

Nina's voice became shrill. "Elizabeth, are you even listening to me?"

"Yes, of course," Elizabeth insisted. "You were going to tell me about some guy?"

"I was?" Nina challenged her. "And do you happen to remember this guy's name?"

"Jim, right?" Elizabeth said.

"It's actually Josh, and I don't suppose you remember anything I said about him, do you?" Nina's voice trembled with irritation.

Elizabeth's shoulders slumped. No, she didn't. But she couldn't admit that to Nina, and she wasn't ready to admit that she was preoccupied by Sam. "Um, he asked you out?" she tried.

"Oh, man, I don't believe this," Nina huffed.

"You know what, Elizabeth? Why don't you just call me back when you have time to talk, okay? Better yet, see what happens next time *you* want some advice, all right?"

Nina hung up, and Elizabeth stood there with the dead receiver. She sighed, knowing she had to call Nina back and apologize. Maybe it would help to get off her chest what had happened between her and Sam. But then Nina would just accuse her of talking about herself.

Elizabeth put the receiver back in its cradle. She'd call Nina later. Right now she had to find Sam.

She had to let him know that everything would be okay, that she wouldn't expect the world from him. That she only wanted to take things slowly, ease into a relationship.

The important thing was that they belonged together. That's all she wanted him to understand. Elizabeth flew upstairs. Time to hit the shower, then the road.

For the first time ever, Elizabeth Wakefield was about to blow off her morning classes.

"Well, well, if it isn't traitor Jessica. The girl who goes around stealing other people's love interests."

Jessica sighed and looked up to find Neil glaring at her. He grabbed a mug from the cabinet and poured himself a cup of coffee, then leaned against the refrigerator.

"I'm not a traitor, Neil."

"Yeah," he cut her off. "That's why you're going after the guy you know I like. The first guy I've liked in almost a year."

She stared at Neil. His gorgeous gray eyes were filled with a combination of anger and hurt. "I'm not going after him."

"Oh, really? You're just dying to become buds with a random guy you met at our party. A guy that I'm crazy about? Give me a break."

"I'm just trying to do you a favor!" she yelled. "I don't think he's gay, Neil. And I'm trying to prove it before you make a fool out of yourself by coming on to him."

That's true, she thought. *That is all I'm doing. I don't like Jason myself. I don't. I don't.*

Maybe if I repeat it enough times, it'll be true.

"Well, maybe I don't need your kind of favors, Jess," he snapped. "Maybe I think he's worth making a fool out of myself over. Did you ever think of that?"

Jessica stared down at the barely touched plate of pancakes drenched in maple syrup in front of her. She'd suddenly lost her appetite.

She hadn't thought of that. She'd never thought of that at all. Neil must really, really like this guy.

Neil slammed his mug on the counter and stalked out of the kitchen.

She had to give up Jason. That's all there was to it.

Nina stared at the same page she'd been staring at for twenty minutes. Sinuous lines stretched around a rectangle, intermittent triangles indicating the strength and direction of the magnetic field created by an electric current. Normally Nina's discerning eye would have picked out significant patterns, divining the principles underlying the example. Now, however, the lines wiggled and squiggled under her eyes, mocking her inability to concentrate long enough to understand the meaning of the diagram.

Shaking her head, she tried to pay attention. The library was quiet, the temperature comfortable. There was nothing to distract her from the page she was trying to study in her textbook.

She pursed her lips, focusing her eyes on the page with grim determination. No use. Not only could she not figure it out, but she was starting to get a headache. Closing her eyes, she let her head flop back in her chair and tried to relax. But she couldn't stop her mind from going over and over the same unpleasant terrain.

Just last night she had felt like she had her life well under control: She had taken control of the situation with Josh rather than letting him dictate their relationship. She had finished her assignment for English. But then this morning she'd spoken to Elizabeth. Her supposed best friend.

Nina sighed and sat up in her chair. She tried massaging her temples and her brow and began to relax a little. She had never noticed before how sore and tense the muscles in her forehead could get. She had never really noticed that she even *had* muscles in her forehead. But now, pressing with her fingers just above her eyebrows, she could feel a tight, tingling pain like she would get in her abdomen after too many crunches.

Nina felt her throat tighten. She couldn't believe how hurt she still felt over how Elizabeth had treated her earlier.

Nina had come to feel like Elizabeth was almost a sister to her, almost family. And family was supposed to be there, no matter what. But talking to Elizabeth had been about as intimate as asking the operator for a phone number.

Nina laid her head down on the library desk, pressing her tired forehead against the cool, smooth wood. *There's no one,* she thought. *No one I can really count on. No one but myself. Just me, myself, and I.*

But then, Nina supposed, she *was* the reliable type. When Elizabeth had been all torn up over that med-school jerk, Finn, Nina had been there for her, rock solid, looking out for her, watching her back, ready to lend an ear or a shoulder, to do anything at all to get her through that tough time. And Elizabeth had been more than ready to lean on her when she needed to. It was only natural for Nina to assume that Elizabeth would be glad to reciprocate when the need arose on her part.

And I deserve it. I'm not just another friend, darn it! Nina thought grimly, sitting up again and smoothing back her hair. *When Elizabeth was all torn up over Finny-Finn-Finn, she didn't turn to someone else, not even Jessica. She wanted to talk to* me *because she trusts me and she values me.* Well, things just weren't equal between them, she concluded ruefully. And that was going to be another problem. Because Nina was getting a little tired of giving all the time and not getting anything back in return. *I'm a person too,* she thought, *just as much as Elizabeth, and if we're going to be "best friends," she's going to have to realize that.*

But meanwhile Nina was still stuck with her guy problem and whether or not to continue seeing Josh. *Is he a player or not?* she wondered again. Briefly energized by her resentment over Elizabeth's un-friend-like response to her on the phone that morning, she resolved to handle the problem on her own. *You're all you've got now, sister,* she said to herself. *Remember, just me, myself, and I.*

Now, back to magnetic fields. If she could count on nothing else, she could always count on the regularities of the laws of nature and on her own ability to comprehend them. *Because this is me,* Nina thought. *This is what I do best.*

But Nina was just starting to follow the intention behind the diagram when she heard the chair across from hers being pulled out and a person sat down in it in a way that she knew. Knew well. Looking up, she saw Josh there before her. He looked fantastic. A clean, faded denim shirt set off the blue of his eyes. His freshly shaven cheeks shone lightly, setting off his strong, straight jaw. His hair was slicked back a little, not too much, just enough to show off the rugged, masculine line of his head and shoulders. And he had a big, sweet, glad-to-see-you smile on his face, just for her.

"Hi, there," he whispered, leaning forward. "I hope I'm not disturbing you."

Nina could feel herself blushing. "It's all right," she whispered back. "I'm afraid I'm not getting very far anyway."

Josh laughed and leaned farther forward over the desk to look at her book. "I never thought I'd hear *you* say that," he whispered curiously. "Well, I'm glad to see you're just a person like the rest of us." And with that, he peered up at her flirtatiously, his eyes just showing from beneath his long eyelashes.

Nina couldn't help but smile. He smelled so nice too! She didn't know what to say. "Well," she half whispered, half croaked, "I'm just going to have to see the TA tomorrow. I can't make heads or tails of this diagram." She found her head tilting to one side, and suddenly her fingers were playing with a stray strand of hair.

"Maybe a cup of coffee would help," Josh suggested.

"Maybe it would," Nina agreed. *This isn't that hard,* she thought. *I just have to remember what I want.*

"Cappuccino might be better," Josh whispered.

"I like cappuccino," Nina offered. Right now he was saying everything she wanted to hear.

"Did you know I have my own cappuccino machine, right in my dorm room?" Josh asked modestly.

"No, I didn't," Nina answered. "Does it make a good cup?"

"I think you might like it," Josh said, nodding. "I'd be honored if you'd try one."

"I'd be honored if you'd make me one." Nina smiled.

"Well, then," he whispered, standing up, and offered her his hand.

He's apologizing for how he'd acted yesterday morning, Nina realized. *He's being flirtatious and gallant and trying to give me what I want. See, you didn't need anyone's advice to tell you that. You just need your own.* Nina swiftly slid her books into her book bag, stood up, and took Josh's hand in her own. Walking slowly and closely together, they headed toward the glass doors of the reading room. And although her eyes were on the floor beneath them to make sure their feet didn't tangle, Nina couldn't help but notice that most of the faces in the reading room were directed their way. Some of the looks were just interested. But Nina couldn't help but conclude, with some satisfaction, that a few of the girls looked downright jealous. *Eat your hearts out, ladies,* she thought, and wrapped her arm around Josh's.

Chapter
Five

Elizabeth dressed hurriedly in jeans, a white, cropped T-shirt, and her New Balance running shoes. She ran downstairs to grab a piece of fruit from the kitchen.

She didn't want to waste time having breakfast; she was too anxious to get out on the road and start looking for Sam. She found an apple in the fridge to eat in the Jeep and then took one last look into Sam's room—just to make sure he hadn't come home while she was showering and getting dressed.

Elizabeth headed for the front door just as Jessica was coming downstairs. Her sister looked miserable.

"Jess? You okay?" Elizabeth asked, peering at her. *Please say yes so I can rush out of here,* she thought.

Jessica nodded. "Yeah, I'm fine. Just got something on my mind."

"Oh, like stealing your best friend's boyfriend?" Neil snapped as he came down the stairs.

Jessica looked at the floor, and Elizabeth could tell her sister was close to tears.

Oh, man, Elizabeth thought. It was this Jason tug-of-war again. A situation she did not want to get in the middle of.

"Hey, guys, has either of you seen Sam this morning?" Elizabeth asked hopefully.

Jessica shook her head.

"Not in days," Neil said distractedly. "He owes me ten bucks, though, so if you see him, tell him I need it, okay?"

"I'm not stealing anyone's boyfriend!" Jessica suddenly screamed, her blue-green eyes blazing at Neil. "First of all, he's not your boyfriend. And second of all, I'm not even interested in him. I've only been hanging out with him to prove my point!"

Neil rolled his eyes.

Elizabeth had heard enough about this stupid competition for Jason's affection. Didn't anyone else care about Sam's whereabouts?

"You guys!" Elizabeth yelled, looking back and forth between Jessica and Neil. "Could you just please forget about Jason for one minute?"

For a second she had the attention of both of them. "Haven't you heard a word I've said?" she pleaded. "Sam is out there somewhere, God knows where. He's totally broke, so where's he staying? What's he eating? Don't you guys care about him at all?"

Jessica and Neil simultaneously each put their hands on their hips and glared at Elizabeth with expressions of extreme irritation. In unison, they repeated what they had been saying for the past three days: "Elizabeth, Sam can take care of himself."

The two of them looked at each other and laughed. But the break in tension didn't last long. Immediately they resumed their argument over Jason, leaving Elizabeth standing between them like an annoying interference in their all-important debate.

Okay, Elizabeth decided, this was obviously getting her nowhere. And she, for one, wasn't so sure that Sam *could* take care of himself.

Neil sat in his bedroom, still hot from his little blowup with Jessica that morning. Again he found himself staring at the phone, wanting to call Jason but afraid of seeming too eager.

He smiled to himself as he imagined Jessica in the room across the hall, staring at her own phone and trying to muster the same courage to call Jason.

He had to admit, it was pretty ridiculous to be fighting with his best friend over the same guy. Especially when neither one of them was really sure if he was interested in *them*. At least Neil had some advantage over Jessica since he knew that Jason was at least interested in *his* half of the population, if not him in particular. Jason was undoubtedly gay. But still, the doubts kept nagging at the back of his mind.

Neil had to make the next move. He wasn't going to lose Jason lying down. *Winning* him lying down was what he really wanted. Neil picked up the phone and dialed Jason's number. All seven digits.

He felt like a dork calling him up to study together again. But so far that was the only pretense he had of getting together with him. Plus Jason was such a fanatic when it came to academics and he was so obsessed with studying for this econ exam that Neil doubted Jason would be willing to make time for anything *except* studying, at least until after the test.

If only Neil could convince Jason to go out with him *after* studying. Then he might be able to make some progress.

After three rings Jason picked up.

"Hello?"

"Hey, Jason, it's Neil." Neil hoped that Jason didn't sense the nervous tremble in his voice.

"Oh, hey, Neil, how's it going?" He sounded perfectly friendly, which was a big relief to Neil after their last off-kilter phone conversation.

The nervous tremble in Neil's voice was replaced

by an edge of anxious hopefulness. "I was just wondering if you wanted to study together tomorrow before the econ test."

"Well." Jason hesitated. "I think I've mostly got it covered. . . ."

"Oh, um, okay," Neil said. *Idiot!* he yelled at himself. Jason wasn't interested. Clearly.

"But if it would help you out, I guess I could quiz you," Jason added.

Hope dawned. "Yeah, um, that would be great," Neil blurted out. "It'd be a big help for me because you know the material so well. . . . But if it wouldn't help you out, I totally understand. Though quizzing me would definitely keep the info fresh in your head. But if not, no problem, really."

Can you sound any more desperate for a date with this guy? Neil berated himself. *Tone it down, man.*

"No, it's not a problem . . . ," Jason explained. "I just had this vision of going to the library alone. You know, going to my secret study spot and banging out some problems. So now I just have to sort of alter my mental agenda, that's all. But if you really want to study together, sure, let's do it."

"Cool!" Neil caught himself sounding a little too enthusiastic and tried to rein himself in before he attempted to expand their little study plans into something more. "Then maybe after we study for a few hours, we can go get a beer or something?"

So much for reining himself in.

"A beer? Before the test?" Jason sounded like Neil had just offered him heroin or something. "Hmmm . . ."

There was a long pause.

Oh, great, Neil thought, *this is when he tells me that maybe we shouldn't study together after all. And that he's not a homo like me and I should just stop calling him.*

God, maybe Jessica was right after all.

Finally Jason spoke again. "A beer, huh? Yeah, maybe that's a good idea. We've been spending so much time studying lately, it might be a good way to take the edge off. As long as we stick to splitting one. Can you imagine trying to take that exam drunk?"

Neil laughed. "Why don't I stop by your place around noon tomorrow?"

"Sounds great, Neil," Jason answered with genuine exuberance. "I'll see you then."

"Cool. See ya, Jason." Neil hung up the phone. Score!

Elizabeth made her way through the concrete campus of OCC as if in a dream. The buildings were all alien and alike, and no face was familiar. She was so stressed out, it was like she was in an alternate reality.

She pictured herself going up to students and asking if they knew Sam Burgess. But she knew it was no use. Judging from all the hours Sam logged on the living-room couch—or *used* to anyway—she doubted he hung out much on campus after classes.

She had a dim memory of his friend Bugsy mentioning that he lived in one of the off-campus dorms, but which one? Besides, she didn't know his friends well enough to hunt them down and ask them questions. All she'd really ever heard about them was vague stories from Sam about playing darts and drinking beer. Anyway, she doubted that Sam let his so-called friends keep better tabs on him than his housemates.

Elizabeth was beginning to think that coming to OCC wasn't such a great idea after all. She knew that Sam had classes on Mondays, but she had no idea what ones or which buildings they were in.

Elizabeth sat down on a concrete bench and dropped her head in her hands. She'd spent an hour wandering around the campus, and once again she'd come up empty.

She took a deep breath and headed back to her car, her eyes peeled in every direction just in case he suddenly appeared. *Yeah, right,* Elizabeth thought as she pulled open the door to the Jeep. *Like he's suddenly going to materialize.*

Elizabeth got back in her car and drove on. To

where, she had no idea. She just drove. Around and around. In circles. Clueless.

This was so unlike her. Usually when Elizabeth focused on achieving an outcome, she knew exactly what to do. She set out a rational plan and stuck to it until she ultimately succeeded. But usually whatever problem she faced didn't involve getting inside the head of Sam Burgess. And that's exactly what she had to do. She had to think like Sam.

Maybe I already am thinking like Sam, Elizabeth pondered. *That would explain why I've been driving around in circles.*

Trying to figure out where she might find Sam made Elizabeth realize just how little she actually knew about him. What *did* he do with all his time? Other than sit around the house and watch television, play video games, and occasionally study, what did he ever actually do?

The one place where she ever heard him talk about hanging out was Frankie's, the bar where her ex-boyfriend Todd Wilkins worked. She knew he liked to play darts there and drink beer with his buddies. Frankie's also happened to be the place where Sam caught Finn Robinson out with another girl, when he supposedly wanted to be monogamous with Elizabeth.

Elizabeth thought back on the whole Finn fiasco and couldn't believe herself. How could she have seen anything in that creep? That liar! How could she have ever considered giving up her virginity to him? And the fact that she had accused Sam of lying when he was only trying to tell her the truth about Finn made Elizabeth's sins all the more reprehensible.

Near sins was more like it, Elizabeth corrected herself, reminding herself again that she never actually slept with Finn. Thanks in part to Sam. Thinking of Finn Robinson made Elizabeth appreciate Sam even more.

Even if he did hold some things back about his family and his private life and even if she didn't necessarily know everything about him, at least he wasn't a big liar like Finn. At least he wasn't out there presenting himself as someone he wasn't.

Elizabeth dreaded going to Frankie's. The thought of being in the same place where Finn had cheated on her made her ill. Plus she didn't exactly want to run into Todd Wilkins either. When she thought about it, though, Frankie's probably wasn't open anyway. It was barely afternoon on a Monday. And besides, Sam wasn't the type to be getting drunk in a dark tavern in the middle of the day. At least, she hoped not. No, Sam would more likely be nursing his hangover from the night before than out getting wasted again.

Suddenly Elizabeth felt a magnetic pull toward the ocean. Of course, the beach! That's exactly where Sam would have gone this time of day to work out his problems. And Elizabeth still believed that wherever Sam was, he was no doubt pondering the Kiss, just as she had been doing these past five days, and what it meant to their relationship. And what better place to think than at the beach?

Elizabeth imagined that Sam was surfing a huge wave or lying out on the sand, deep in thought about their future, right now. As she drove westward Elizabeth realized that perhaps her search for Sam was really a distraction from her own thoughts about the Kiss and the future of their relationship. She wondered if she even knew what she would say to him if and when she found him. Maybe she really didn't want to think about all this. And maybe she didn't want to know what Sam thought.

What if to Sam, their kiss meant the end? Or worse yet, what if it meant nothing at all?

Still, she needed to find out. She needed to find Sam. She needed to talk to him. She needed to listen.

Elizabeth had been driving west for only a couple of miles when something caught her eye. Sam's car! His clunky old eyesore stuck out like a sore thumb among all the luxury sedans and SUVs that filled the parking lot to her left. That's why she had been able to notice it from the road.

But what would Sam's car be doing in the parking

lot of the Sweet Valley Resort Hotel? And more important, what would Sam be doing inside?

She knew he couldn't afford a room there unless he had some rich uncle he had never told her about. And she doubted Sam had taken a job as a bellhop. As far as Elizabeth knew, Sam hadn't worked a day in his life and didn't plan to in the immediate future.

Maybe it wasn't even Sam's car at all. Well, whether it was or it wasn't, Elizabeth had to find out. She turned her car around and headed into the parking lot. As she pulled up behind the car, there was no doubt about it. It had the same dent in the back and the same dumb bumper sticker: My Kid Beats Up Honor-Roll Students.

Plus it would have been just like Sam to park in the spot marked Owner. She was surprised he hadn't been towed away. *Maybe he just got here,* she thought. *Maybe he's trying to sneak into the pool for a swim and a hot shower.*

Whatever was going on, Elizabeth was about to find out.

Nina and Josh walked into his dorm room together, the door swinging gently shut behind them. It looked like he'd cleaned the place up a little. The shelves and the desk were free of dust, and the industrial-grade carpet had a freshly vacuumed appearance. Nina noticed that Josh's bed was neatly made, with a blue flannel bedspread that she didn't remember seeing the first time she'd been in his room. She felt pleased to be here and very happy to be with Josh at all. There she had been, alone in the library, feeling abandoned by her friends, when up had walked this cute guy, all shoulders and eyelashes, looking just for her, wanting to be with her, wanting to help make her happy. What was so wrong with that?

Maybe she'd been too hard on him, she thought. He made her feel good about herself, and that was what counted. That was the problem with me, myself, and I—those three got lonely. But with a little lipstick and the right attitude, there was someone else to keep them company.

Nina sat down on Josh's bed while he went over to put on some music. An acoustic guitar strummed, and a man's voice crooned softly. Josh came back over and sat down beside her, taking her by the hand.

"Um, who is this singing?" Nina asked.

"Elliott Smith," Josh answered. "Do you like it?"

"I guess," Nina said. It sounded kind of weird, though, like the singer was in a little pain or something.

"I like him because he's very soulful," Josh murmured, looking into Nina's eyes. "His singing makes me think of you. The way I feel around you." He stroked her hand with his and looped his other arm around her shoulders.

"That's nice," Nina said softly, suddenly self-conscious. She liked Josh's romantic nature, but why did he have to come on so strong? After all, they'd just walked into the room. She wanted to believe that he really liked her and wasn't just trying to have sex with her, but he was making it hard. He wasn't as charming and playful as he had been in the library. He was just sitting quietly, listening to the music and stroking her palm. Nina started to feel more uncomfortable.

For one thing, Elliott Smith was starting to sound like he really had to go to the bathroom or had something in his eye, and it was making his voice go off-key.

Nina asked, "Um, do you think we could listen to something else? Something, I don't know, happier?"

Josh looked a little irritated. "Sure," he said. "Whatever you want."

He went back to the CD player. Soon Jennifer Lopez was singing to a lively beat about how long she'd been waiting for tonight. And Josh was back beside her on the bed, one arm around her shoulders, the other tracing circles in her palm. Nina found it easier to relax. The gentle stroking in her hand felt beautiful, and she liked the music's slinky beat. This wasn't so bad! A girl could get used to it.

Josh spoke very softly now, his lips just a few inches from her ear. "Nina," he said. "I feel so different about you. . . . I don't know what it is. You're so different from the other girls around here! You're not just smart, and pretty, but you have everything so together. I really respect that . . . the way you're so confident. I really feel like I can just be myself around you. And that's very special, a very special thing."

Nina could feel the blood rising to her face. She liked hearing these words. She liked the romantic attention. She began feeling very relaxed, and the complex world of SVU receded in her mind. The gentle stroking in her palm began to have an almost hypnotic effect. So soft, and regular, and persistent, but not intrusive. If only they could sit like this for a while, just easy and nonthreatening, she thought, she could definitely be happy about it.

Josh was almost whispering. "Oh, you smell so nice. Like a field of wildflowers! It's making me dizzy. Your hand is so smooth and small. You feel so good to me. You have the most beautiful skin. It's irresistible."

Nina felt her eyes closing, and she let her head fall to rest on Josh's wide shoulder. Then she could feel his weight shift and his head move closer to hers. Next the soft touch of his lips was brushing across her neck. Nina shivered, the goose bumps rising all over.

Josh's lips were tracing feathers on her neck, softly, sweetly. Nina could feel the blood rushing into her face, feel her senses heighten, becoming electric. Time began to slow for her, the beat of the music, the pulse of her own heart. She felt Josh's lips part over her neck, and he gently began to kiss her there in small, slow caresses.

Nina clutched his hand tightly and let her head drop farther. Josh let go of her hand and clasped her other shoulder, holding her firmly but gently. His kisses grew more passionate, wider, harder. Nina felt the wet warmth of his tongue pressing occasionally against the sensitive skin of her neck, adding another thrill to the pleasure of his touch. He was so sensitive, so passionate. "Josh," she murmured. "Oh, Josh . . ."

"Nina," he said against her neck. "Sweet Nina." And then his lips began a path of kisses over her jaw and cheek to find their way to her lips, like a little animal seeking its nest in the dark. He captured her mouth in his and pulled gently against her lips, moistening them, softly holding them between his, his tongue pressing against them. It felt fantastic. So good. Too good! Too fast!

Nina pushed her hands against Josh's shoulders. His grip was tight, though, and he continued to kiss her. "Josh!" Nina said, half muffled by his kisses.

"Mmmm?" he replied, still kissing her.

"Josh . . . ," she repeated, pushing a little harder against his shoulders. She closed her mouth. Enough!

"What is it, Nina?" He sounded gently concerned. He allowed his hands to fall, and one took hers.

"What about that cappuccino?" she asked brightly. "I think one might be perfect just about now."

He looked incredulous. "Right," he said. "Coffee." Standing up, he crossed the small room to a cabinet above his desk. Reaching up and shuffling among its contents, he managed to extract the bulky black device. Next a bag emerged, and he produced a packet of finely ground coffee, a spoon, packets of sugar, and some small black plastic parts to the machine. "Coming right up, *Signora*," he trilled, his teeth flashing as he smiled. *"Un cappuccino, presto!"*

A bottle of water was poured into the reservoir. A pint of milk was pulled from the tiny dorm fridge. The machine was plugged into the wall, and small red lights began to glow. A small metal cup with a handle was filled with coffee and wrenched into place. A demitasse cup was positioned underneath. Josh whistled tunelessly, moving his rump from side to side in a happy little dance.

Nina couldn't help but giggle as she watched him in his task. He really was too cute. And it really did seem like he would do anything for her. Maybe she had gotten him wrong. Maybe she was paranoid now, after the burnout with Xavier. *Not every guy is like Xavier,* she thought. *Give the guy a chance! Have a little fun. Let him entertain you. Just don't sleep with him! Not till you're sure he's willing to commit to a relationship.*

Something was wrong with the coffee machine. When Josh pressed a certain button, it seemed like something significant should happen, but all that happened was that a weak trickle of water seeped out, dripping on his desk. He frowned, and jiggled the handles, and checked the various connections. No good. Once again mere seepage. No coffee. No steam. Josh looked the device over to no avail. He began to look glum.

"I don't think it's working," he said ruefully. "It did this before, and I had to bring it back to the dealer to get it fixed. Oh, I don't know."

Nina felt sorry for him. He seemed pretty embarrassed.

He sat down in his desk chair and looked at her frankly. "Great. Now you're gonna think I lied about making you a cup, right? I swear I didn't," he said, looking miserable. "I know I acted like a jerk yesterday morning, but I didn't mean to, Nina. I was just, I don't know, nervous, I guess. About stuff happening so fast. Does that sound lame?"

Nina smiled. "No. Not at all. That's what I thought. About yesterday, I mean. I think we should take things slowly too, Josh. So neither of us has anything to get uptight about anymore, okay?"

He smiled at her so genuinely that Nina wanted to jump up and wrap her arms around him.

See, guys and girls aren't so different after all, she reflected. *He's scared, you're scared. Everyone's just scared. Of getting hurt, of getting burned. Of showing who they really are.*

"We could go to Yum-Yum's for cappuccino if you really want one," she said. "Whatever you want, my treat."

Nina stood up. She didn't need the coffee anyway. She was plenty pumped up and was having no trouble concentrating. And she didn't want to leave this guy for a hot beverage. He was sweeter than any coffee anyway, she mused, and she didn't want to let him out of her hands. Crossing over the small room, she reached over to the machine and turned it off. It gurgled in defeat.

Josh looked up to where she stood before him, a sweet and helpless look on his face. Nina curled her hand behind his neck and lowered her lips to his. She kissed him fully, deeply, and passionately. He returned her embrace with hot and hungry kisses. She felt his hands on the backs of her knees and then climbing the backs of her thighs. She stepped closer to him and then sat down on his lap, straddling him on his chair, their bodies pressed close together. She shut her eyes and kissed him more passionately than before. *Mmmm, nice,* she thought. *Just right. Just me and Josh. Sweet.*

Chapter
Six

_____

Elizabeth strode purposefully through the gleaming lobby of the Sweet Valley Resort Hotel and approached the front desk. She doubted that the buttoned-down check-in clerk would have any idea who Sam Burgess was, but she figured it was worth a try. Maybe he really had gotten a job there. Or for all she knew, maybe he really did have a rich uncle who was putting him up. *Putting up with him would be more like it.* Elizabeth chuckled to herself. But she knew there was no way Sam had a rich *anything*. The guy was perpetually broke. He'd once told Elizabeth that he'd chosen OCC because they'd offered him a scholarship and because he was totally on his own as far as paying his way.

After standing in line for less than a minute (Elizabeth knew that at fancy hotels like this, they never liked to make their guests wait), she walked up and was greeted by the attendant as if her jeans-and-T-shirt outfit was a hundred percent Prada. "Good afternoon, madame. How may I help you?"

"Actually, I'm looking for a young man named Sam Burgess." Elizabeth spoke uncertainly.

The man behind the counter glanced down at his computer terminal and announced with a hint of surprise, "Why, you're in luck. Mr. Burgess just happens to be in today."

"*Mr.* Burgess?" Elizabeth was taken aback. She had never in her life heard Sam referred to as a mister. In fact, she had never even imagined it.

"Yes, room twelve," he answered matter-of-factly. "Is he expecting you?"

The strangeness of this whole experience was overwhelming, but somehow Elizabeth managed to think on her toes. Of course he wasn't expecting her; *she* wasn't even expecting to find *him* here. But now that she had, she thought it was best to surprise him. That way if he did happen to be avoiding her, he wouldn't have an opportunity to escape.

"Er, yes, he is expecting me," Elizabeth answered, sure that her confusion was totally transparent. "Room twelve, you say?"

"Yes, room twelve. Straight down that hallway, and take the elevator to floor one." The clerk pointed the way and then signaled the end of their transaction by shifting his eye contact to the next person in line.

This is just too weird, Elizabeth thought as she walked toward the elevator. *"Mr. Burgess?" "Happens to be in?"* She just didn't get it. But she guessed that everything would make sense soon enough.

On the way up, Elizabeth smiled awkwardly at the well-heeled guests sharing her elevator. She was suddenly self-conscious about her casual attire. But how could she have possibly predicted that she would have found herself in the Sweet Valley Resort Hotel today?

When Elizabeth finally reached the room—or rather, the suite—she was taken aback once again. For one thing, the door was fancier than every other one on the hall. And for another, it was posted with a plaque that said Owner's Suite.

This was just too much. There had to be a mistake. She wasn't about to just knock on the door of the owner's suite at the Sweet Valley Resort Hotel, looking for Sam Burgess. There was no way she was going to find him inside that room.

At the risk of upsetting some grand scheme Sam might be pulling off at the hotel—like sneaking into the pool or perhaps an elaborate towel-laundering operation—Elizabeth returned to the front desk to make sure that she and the attendant were talking about the same Sam Burgess.

The clerk recognized her as soon as she returned. "Is there a problem?" he asked respectfully.

"Um, I don't know. I think there might have been some mistake."

"A mistake?" he asked quizzically. "What sort of mistake?"

"Well, there's a plaque on the door of room twelve that says Owner's Suite," Elizabeth answered, with an equal measure of confusion in her voice.

"You did say you were looking for Mr. Burgess, did you not?"

"Yes, *Sam* Burgess," Elizabeth clarified.

"Yes, of course," he replied calmly. "Mr. Samuel Burgess owns the hotel."

"Owns the hotel?" Elizabeth could barely contain her disbelief.

"Precisely." The clerk appeared to be losing patience. "That is why Mr. Burgess is in the *owner's suite*."

"Wait a second. Are we talking about the same Mr. Sam Burgess here? The one I'm looking for is nineteen years old, sandy brown hair, dressed like a college student, probably wearing jeans and a T-shirt?"

"Yes, that's him," the clerk answered slowly, as if speaking to a child.

Huh? Elizabeth thought. *Could there be two Sam Burgesses that match that description?*

There was only one way to find out.

Neil walked into Jessica's room with a giant smile spread across his face. He couldn't wait to tell her about the study date he had planned with Jason for tomorrow afternoon.

Jessica was dressed in tight jeans and an ice blue tank top. She was staring at herself in the full-length mirror on her closet door.

"You look great as usual," he called from the doorway.

Jessica glanced back, embarrassed. "Haven't you ever heard of knocking, Neil?"

"Hmmm . . . knocking. I'm not sure." Neil played dumb. "Isn't that the thing you do when a door is *closed*?"

"Just because my door was open doesn't give you the right to sneak up on me like that." Jessica's good-cheer resources had evidently been depleted.

Neil got defensive. "I wasn't sneaking up on you. I just wanted to tell you something."

"Oh, let me guess," Jessica started. "You and Jason have another little study date planned."

"Whoa, how'd you guess?" Neil was incredulous.

"Why else would you rush in here gloating like this?" Jessica let out a huge sigh. "Especially since last time I saw you, you were trying to tear my head off."

"Oh, come on," Neil protested. "You know I'd never try to hurt you. You do know that, Jess, right?"

Jessica faked a sniffle. "You *do* hurt me, Neil, *inside*."

"So, now who's the drama queen, huh?" Neil teased. "Do I sense a bit of jealousy, Jessica?"

"What's there to be jealous about?" Jessica was obviously trying to sound nonchalant. "I mean, like you said, you have a *study* date. That is, with the emphasis on *study*."

"Oh, yeah?" Neil challenged her. "Well, what if I told you that we also have plans to go get drinks afterward? So I'd have to say the emphasis is shifting undeniably toward *date*."

"Drinks?" Jessica scoffed. "Jason doesn't drink. What, is he taking you out for ginkgo-biloba cocktails or something?"

"For your information, the word he used was *beer*," Neil answered smugly. "He said that after all the studying we've done, it might help take the edge off."

"I stand corrected," Jessica answered stiffly.

Neil studied Jessica's face. "You really *are* jealous, aren't you?"

"Neil." Jessica softened her tone. "The reason I'm not jealous is because there's nothing to be jealous about. If anything, I'm concerned for *you*."

"Oh, right," Neil huffed. "You're concerned for me. That's a good one. Well, you know what? I'm going to be just fine, okay? Especially after tomorrow afternoon."

"Oh?" Jessica gave her head an added tilt. "And what's so special about tomorrow, besides it being another one of your little study dates? Oh, I almost forgot. You and Jason are getting *beers* afterward. Oooooh."

"The beers are going to be just the beginning," Neil answered suggestively.

"Oh, really," Jessica remarked.

"Yes, really." Neil took a deep breath. He wasn't sure telling Jessica about his plan was the best idea. But he felt he had to tell someone, if for no other reason than to make it more real. Not just something inside his head. Somehow saying it out loud would make it impossible for him to chicken out.

"Because this afternoon," he continued after a long pause, "I promised myself that I'm going to finally make the first move."

"Listen, Neil." Jessica suddenly assumed her Elizabeth persona. "I really am concerned for you. I know I've told you this before, but I guess I'm just going to have to keep repeating myself until you understand. Jason is not gay. He does not like men. You know that the only reason I went after him in the first place was to prove that to you. So let me say this one more time: As soon as you lean in and try to kiss him, I swear to God, your whole fantasy is going to come crashing down. And you're the one who's going to be humiliated, Neil. So you can promise yourself whatever you want. But I just think you need to think about the consequences."

Neil was so fed up with Jessica's colossal ego. The nerve of her pretending to look out for *his* best interests when he knew the only person she really cared about was Jessica Wakefield! It was so painfully obvious she was trying to get Neil out of the picture so she could have Jason for herself.

"You are so full of it, Jessica!" Neil shouted. "Since when are you the expert on gay America? If anyone knows whether Jason is gay or straight, it's me. I can sense these things, okay?"

"Yeah, whatever," Jessica muttered dismissively.

"Your ego is getting a little hard to take, you know that?" Neil screamed. "Why can't you just admit it? You like Jason more than you care about our friendship! Isn't that right?"

Jessica narrowed her eyes at Neil and spoke in a subdued voice. "You know what, Neil? Go right ahead. Go ahead and waste your first move in forever on a guy who's straight. Make a fool of yourself. Prove me right. Fine. Go ahead."

"Fine, I will," Neil said.

Jessica glared at him. "Fine."

"Fine." Neil wasn't exactly sure what he had expected to happen when he walked into Jessica's room, but it certainly wasn't another fight. Well, until things with Jason sorted themselves out, he guessed that there could be no peace between him and his supposed best friend.

And at this point there wasn't much more he could say except "fine" again.

And with that, Neil turned and walked out the door.

Sam sat beside Anna on the king-size bed, leafing through the newspaper and absentmindedly nibbling on a grape from the brunch tray. He had to admit, the lap of luxury wasn't so bad after all. Unfortunately his quiet moment of bliss was interrupted by a sharp knock at the door.

"Hey," Anna spoke up, smiling. "Did you order massages for us after all while I was in the shower?"

"Um, no," Sam answered as he slid off the bed and padded over to the door in his bare feet and boxers. "I wonder who it is."

Sam pulled open the door, and his instantaneous expression of shock was mirrored on the face in front of him.

Elizabeth.

Sam's jaw dropped just as Elizabeth's did.

Finally Elizabeth broke the stunned silence. "Your family owns this hotel?"

Sam nodded slowly. What could he say?

Anna's voice cut in from behind him. "Who's at the door, honey?" she asked playfully.

Elizabeth leaned in to see who was speaking.

Oh, man. This was about to get worse.

Worse than Sam could have ever imagined.

The only time Elizabeth had met Anna was when Sam had paraded Anna past Elizabeth as a one-night stand, a sexual conquest. It had been totally staged, of course, with Anna deserving an Academy Award for the role as "used girl." Sam had wanted to prove to Elizabeth that a guy could act like he liked a girl, sleep with her, and then lose interest totally once he had what he wanted. It was all in the name of stopping Elizabeth from losing her virginity to Finn.

So he and Anna had played their parts. So well, in fact, that Elizabeth had bought it hook, line, and sinker. She'd been disgusted by what Sam had done to "poor Anna." But it had only furthered her idea of *him* as a jerk. It hadn't worked on all guys. In fact, it might have pushed her farther into Finn Robinson's arms.

Now he watched Elizabeth's expression change from shock to pain and back to shock. He knew she recognized Anna. And that she was mistakenly assuming that he had slept with Anna last night. The girl was, after all, in his hotel room and wearing a bathrobe.

Elizabeth's beautiful blue-green eyes shone with tears. She looked at him, then her face crumpled before his eyes.

Speechless, she turned from Sam and sprinted down the hallway toward the elevator.

Trembling, Sam stood there for a moment, then slowly closed the door after her. He turned to face Anna.

"What are you doing?" Anna shrieked. "Aren't you going to go after her?"

"No," Sam said.

Anna was incredulous. "What?"

"Didn't you see her face?" he asked. "She hates me now. She won't want to talk to me ever again."

Anna stared at him. "Sam, don't be an idiot. Go after her!"

Sam took a deep breath and dropped down on the sofa. "I'm not going after her, Anna. It's probably better that this happened anyway."

Anna's mouth dropped open. "That *what* happened? That Elizabeth found you shacked up in some fancy hotel with some girl she last met as your one-night-stand?"

Sam bowed his head. "Yeah."

"Omigod," Anna said. "I cannot believe you."

Sam let out a deep breath and glanced up at his friend. He'd never seen her so angry. "What?" he snapped. "It's my business, Anna, not yours. I don't need this from you, okay?"

"Sam, you've probably got one second to go after her before she drives away. I'd go if I were you."

"Well, you're *not* me," he barked. "I'm not going after her. Now she knows I've been lying about my family—"

Sam glanced at Anna. He'd never told her the real story about his family. He'd never lied; he'd simply never talked about the Burgesses.

Anna leveled a glare at him. "Forget me, Sam. Just go on. I'm dying to hear your reasoning for letting Elizabeth go."

Sam shook his head. "It's just that I've never told her or anyone that I come from one of the richest families in Boston. I've acted like I'm this broke guy from a poor family. But, um, as you heard, Anna, my family's anything but poor. They own this hotel. *I* sort of own this hotel."

"Sam, I'm gonna save the fact that you kept that information from me too for another time and place. Right now I want to know why you're not going after her. How could you let her think we slept together? I'll bet seeing me here broke her heart just then."

"Maybe that's not such a terrible thing," he said. "Maybe it's better that she thinks I'm scum and saves herself the trouble of getting involved with me."

"And this is good because?" Anna asked, in a tone of utter confusion.

"Because I'm only gonna hurt her," Sam explained, leaning back against the sofa. "This way we'll go back to the way it was before. Fighting. Arguing. She'll think I'm a jerk, and she'll keep her distance, and then I won't have to worry about avoiding *her*. Everything will go back to how it was before that stupid kiss."

"You are such an idiot!" Anna screamed.

"What?" Sam asked. "Why are you getting so bent out of shape? You're supposed to be on my side."

Anna hurriedly got dressed as she launched a tirade against Sam. "After everything we talked about last night, you still don't get it, do you? You know, I don't think you deserve Elizabeth after all. And I know for a fact she doesn't deserve a jackass like you!"

Sam stared at her.

"I cannot believe you!" Anna shrieked, working herself into a frenzy. "How can you hurt her like that? You really must not care about anyone, Sam, if you can treat the girl you're in love with that way."

"Those were your words, Anna," he yelled back at her. "I never said I was in love with Elizabeth. You did."

"You're a child, Sam. You're a scared little kid who's afraid of a real relationship. You're afraid of intimacy. And you know what? It's not that you're afraid to hurt her. You're afraid she's gonna hurt *you*."

"Whatever," Sam shot back belligerently. "It's none of your business anyway. It's about me and her. What's the big deal to you?"

Anna pulled on her jacket and rushed toward the door. "The big deal is that you're not the kind of guy I thought you were. You're a selfish, insensitive child who only cares about himself. And that's not the kind of guy I want to know. Good-bye."

Anna slammed the door behind her, leaving Sam alone. In the lap of luxury. To wonder to himself what the hell had just happened.

Chapter Seven

In her dream Nina was trapped in a room with many doors and windows. She knew she had to get somewhere important, to free herself from a fearful presence that beset her, but somehow, she knew, she was doomed to taking the wrong path. All the doors were wrong: One would lead to the cold outdoors, from which she would never reemerge; one would lead her into a maze; one would take her back the way she had come; and so on, for every one of them.

Beginning to panic, she spun around in the room. *Surprise them,* she thought. *Do something none of them would expect. Something completely different.* Eyeing a tall window, she took in its long, velvet drapes, spilling chaotically over the floor at its base. Steeling her resolve, Nina ran to the window and flung open the French doors. Beneath her a beautiful fountain splashed musically among marble statuary. She could smell the humidity as of a greenhouse: Looking up, she could see that the ceiling was composed of panes of green glass. Delicate tendrils of ivy swayed gently in the sweet air. Somewhere a parrot cawed.

Quick, now, Nina told herself. *Don't let them see you thinking about it. Just go! Everything will be all right. There's nothing that can follow you down there, and once you reach the floor, you'll be safe among the statues.*

She grabbed the long drapes firmly, took a deep breath, and jumped into space. Expecting to slide down the drapes to safety, she found herself unable to let them go, and instead she swung back to the wall below the window. In the terrible logic of dreams the drapes now pinned her to the wall, imprisoning her between the soft material and the hard, cold wall.

The more she struggled, the more tightly she was held immobile. Now she couldn't move her arms at all. A panicked frustration welled up inside her. She had to free herself! In trying to escape, she had bound herself more firmly than she would have been had she allowed herself to be captured in the first place. Fear and self-reproach made her body tense and shake. Abandoning herself to her terror, she tried to scream, but nothing came out of her mouth.

She began to flail violently, doing whatever she could to get out of the clutches of the soft curtain that held her against the immobile wall beside her. She wanted to cry.

With a wrenching psychic burst, Nina surfaced to waking consciousness. Opening her eyes, her heart pounding, sweating, her mouth dry, she found herself wrapped in a blanket, smashed against a wall. She had no idea where she was, but anything was better than her dream prison. She slowly loosed her grip on the blanket and relaxed her neck, easing her face away from the smooth wall, and tried to breathe. *Oh, thank goodness,* she thought. *I'm all right. Everything is all right.*

As she woke up fully, she realized where she was. Josh's room. His little hard dorm bed. She rolled over to see him sleeping beside her, sprawled over his bed, his arms and legs akimbo, a thin strand of drool joining his mouth to his pillow. Gross.

He must have pushed her against the wall, and she had gotten tangled in the flannel blanket. Her heart slowed to a normal pace, and she felt her tongue recede in her mouth, becoming mobile again. Putting her hand to her damp forehead, she reviewed the night's events and groaned inwardly.

Well, she thought. *So much for waiting. So much for getting to know each other. You did it, girl. Sex.*

Now you've had sex with him. And what's going to happen now? Ohhhh.

Moving gently so as not to wake Josh, Nina pulled her body into a half-sitting position. She spread the blanket gently over Josh's bare body. Then, with a gymnast's dexterity, she eased one leg over his prone figure to the floor and, shifting her weight slowly, raised herself to her feet beside his bed. Her naked skin gathered goose bumps in the dawn chill. Outside Josh's window the early light played among the buildings and grounds of Sweet Valley University. The campus was deserted of people, but birds were flitting from tree to tree, and squirrels were dashing among the bushes, dodging the papers that swirled in the breeze.

Nina reached for her T-shirt and pulled it over her head. Then she couldn't find her underwear. After a careful search of the floor she reasoned that they must still be in the bed, where Josh had pulled them from her the previous night. With chagrin Nina searched with her hands around the sheet that lay in a jumble at the foot of the bed.

She had meant to keep clothed and to leave after a little while. But his persistent tugging at her shirt had convinced her—what's the harm?—to remove it. His delicate touch on her breasts, first through her bra and then under it, had persuaded her to let him take it off. But she was going to keep her pants on! Nothing below the waist! So much for good intentions, though.

She had enjoyed his touch, Nina thought, but that wasn't the main impetus behind her acquiescence. It was more the security she felt in giving him what he wanted. When he touched her thighs and then more intimately, first through her pants, and then under her waistband, and then, daringly, seductively, unbuttoning and unzipping, she had felt a sweet delight and comfort in the very fact of his desire for her, the slowness with which he moved, the way he continued to kiss and caress her, constantly providing her with pleasure and warmth.

The strangeness between them, the fact that they hadn't really talked about much but classes and superficial things, that they didn't even know much about each other, had hardly shared more than a few moments, faded into obscurity as their physical communication brought them closer and closer on a nonverbal level, a plane of physical intimacy. And then over time, as they lay close together, Nina had come to feel such a deep affection for Josh, such a placid sense of ease and lassitude, that she had come just to accept him as he was, to accept what was between them as meaningful, as right, as true.

When he lay on top of her, and she was at the last stage when she could still tell him to stop, she took such pleasure from his pleasure, such a sweet delight in the happiness she knew she could give him, that she wanted him to go further, wanted to take him all the way. She had wanted him; there was no doubt about it. It wasn't like she was in a swoon: At some point, when she could sense that he was growing uncomfortable, that he was giving her a chance to say that that was enough, she had decided, had really consciously, deliberately decided, that she wanted him completely. She had taken his chin in her hands and asked him if he had a condom. And of course he had.

Nina located her underwear among the twists of the discarded sheet. If she could only get dressed quietly, she could get out of there before he woke up. After the cold way he had treated her in his room on Sunday morning, she didn't want to give him a chance to upset her again. She could leave him a little note and get herself home to think about what she had done and what she was going to do next. With a pang, the sense of loss she had experienced over Elizabeth's inconsideration revisited her.

She was just going to have to figure this one out for herself. And it wasn't going to be easy. For a moment she almost panicked, feeling lost and abandoned in her suddenly complicated world. She did a little dance to get her underwear over her knees. She pulled them on. She stepped on the cold, slimy condom lying on the floor. It was disgusting. She wanted to cry. Her body began to crumple slightly, her knees bending and her belly quivering, and she had to sit down for a moment, trying to perch on the edge of the iron bedstead so as not to jar Josh awake. She reached underneath the bed to find her bra.

Too late. Josh was awake. Nina could feel him stir behind her, rolling over on his side. She tensed up, preparing herself not to worry about what he said, focusing on getting herself dressed and out of there. She found her bra with her fingers and quickly pulled it underneath her T-shirt to put it on. But Josh's arms were curling around her waist, and she could feel his cheek pressed against her lower back. She couldn't pull her T-shirt up enough to reach the bra through the armhole. She found herself wishing that he would just be cold enough again to let her get dressed quickly.

This was no time to pay attention to details. If he was going to drop her now, to not call, to pretend that nothing had happened between them, then let him. *What's happened has happened*, Nina thought, *and there's nothing to be done about it now. And it's all right. You don't need this guy, and you can sleep with whomever you want, and you were careful about the condom, and you have a lot of studying to do for electricity and magnetism today, and if you let yourself get upset about some dumb guy, you're not going to be able to do it. And there are other guys, and you'll find a good one sooner or later. It doesn't matter; it's like it never happened.*

Nina was like a person who had fallen off a boat and was concentrating on only one thing: survival. And for her survival meant getting dressed. But Josh wasn't really letting her. First he had been holding her around the waist, and now he was caressing her from behind, his soft hands tracing patterns on her arms and legs, his face rubbing against her back. It felt nice. It felt *very* nice. Nina was torn. What had been the cruel sea was turning into a warm bath.

"Hey, lover," she heard his voice from behind her. "What's your hurry?"

Nina allowed her stiff body to relax. The sense of emergency began to subside. Maybe she could take her time a little, just tell him she had to go, that he could go back to sleep. She still didn't have to give him a chance to be a dork, but she didn't have to be sneaky about getting out of there. "Oh, nothing," she whispered. "I just have a lot to do today."

"Nina, darling, you're so good, so dedicated," Josh murmured, kissing her back through her shirt and then, sitting up more, finding the back of her neck with his soft lips. Nina shivered electrically at the touch of his mouth on her neck. He found her earlobe and sucked it gently, his hands roaming freely and delicately over her thighs, creeping under her shirt and pulling her back against him.

"But it isn't even six o'clock!" Now he was bringing his legs out from underneath himself and holding her hips between his strong thighs. He grasped her chest with one arm and with the other took her by the jaw to turn her face sideways. He kissed her gently on the ear, and Nina felt her goose bumps heighten and then subside. Where she had felt cold, she now was feeling warm. Where she had felt fear, she was now feeling safety and comfort in his touch. She softened inside and closed her eyes.

His touch was so gentle, so calm, so accepting of her as his hand traced her curves through her shirt and then grasped her firmly, pulling her to him more closely. Her back was pressed hard against him, and she could feel his passion intensely. Suddenly she wanted him again, wanted that happy, forgetful oneness that she had craved the night before.

He pulled his mouth away from her ear and whispered incredibly softly, so that she could barely hear him, although his lips were a fraction of an inch from her moist, throbbing ear. "Why don't you stay awhile? We could . . . um . . . you know, hang out"—a dart of the tongue—"and then maybe get some breakfast, hmmm? I promise you'll be in the library when it opens at nine."

Just then Nina felt better about Josh than she

ever had. He was acting like he really liked her, like his passion was just for her, like he wanted to communicate with her inner being through his touch. She felt incredibly excited.

You goose, she said to herself. *You were all afraid for nothing. This is a great guy. This is the one you want. Nina, baby, you've got to give people a chance! Not everyone is like Xavier! Don't be so insecure! It's going to work out just right.* His touch was like magic, sending ripples of pleasure wherever he touched her. Turning around in his lap, she faced him, their bodies pressing together. She pulled her T-shirt off over her head and leaned in for a long, slow, languorous kiss. There was no hurry at all.

Neil carefully laid out three pairs of Levi's and an assortment of six different Calvin Klein T-shirts on top of his bed. He knew he wanted to dress casually, but what to wear, exactly?

White jeans, black jeans, or classic faded denim? The white ones made him feel sexiest, but the black ones suggested going out and the mysteries of night. Since they planned on getting a beer after their study session, maybe black was the way to go. But then again, the tastefully shabby basic-blue 501 jeans conveyed a sense of comfort—of not really caring—that he thought was perfect for a study date and casual drinks. He didn't want to seem like he was trying *too* hard to look good for Jason.

Right, Neil thought, *like I'm not trying too hard. Trying to decide on my outfit six hours before I leave the house? That's just effortless, isn't it?*

The faded blue jeans would go best with the plain white tee, but wasn't that a bit too boring? He had five other ones to choose from. The plain white one definitely screamed out "clean and fresh," which he knew Jason could appreciate. But the plain black crew neck was more understated. And somehow more sophisticated. More New York. But did he want to be "New York" for Jason? After all, both of them were California boys through and through.

He was leaning toward the faded blues with the ribbed gray V neck. Neil thought the combination conveyed a certain relaxed sensuality, with a subtle emphasis on originality.

Planning his wardrobe had served as a calming effect after his most recent spat with Jessica. But now that the selection process was complete, his thoughts drifted back to his meddling housemate. And, Neil was surprised to realize, he was still fuming. What was Jessica's problem anyway?

She is so completely full of herself, Neil thought angrily. *She could have any straight guy on campus, but no, she has to go after the one guy I'm interested in. Some friend. And to think, she says she's going after him just to save me the humiliation of finding out the hard way that he's straight!*

Neil paused from his internal tantrum against Jessica at recalling her final words. Hadn't she said she'd leave Jason alone if that's what he really wanted?

"Jason is all yours."

Isn't that what she had said? Neil began to second-guess his assessment of Jessica's motives. Maybe she really did think that she was looking out for his best interests. *It would be totally like her to think that she's responsible for saving me from heartache. She's so vain, I wouldn't be surprised if Jessica imagined herself to be the savior of the free gay world.*

Again Neil had to laugh at the whole situation. How mad could he be at his best friend for chasing after a guy who was as obviously homosexual as Jason was? And for her to be doing it all out of concern for Neil's feelings made it all the more comical. And in a way, endearing.

The more he thought about the scenario, the more he was able to admit how happy he really was.

Here he was at Sweet Valley University. He had finally met a guy who made him feel like he was ready to start dating again. And he had a best friend who was willing to do anything for him, including making a complete idiot of herself.

Neil was so certain that Jason was gay that he

didn't even care anymore if Jessica wanted to pursue him. If she was so hell-bent on proving to Neil that Jason was straight, let her go ahead and try. She was the one who was going to be humiliated, not Neil.

Jessica sat with a glass of orange juice at the kitchen table, pretending to read the paper. For some reason, she couldn't concentrate. Actually, it was for one very good reason. And his name was Jason Wells.

She couldn't wait another day to see him. But of course she knew she had to. After all, Neil and Jason were having their little study date tonight, and Jessica certainly didn't want to interfere with that. She had made plans to see a movie with Jason tomorrow, so she'd just have to sweat it out for another twenty-four hours or so. But it wasn't going to be easy.

Jessica couldn't get him out of her mind. What was she thinking when she told Neil he could have him? She might have gone after Jason initially as a way to prove to Neil that Jason was straight, but since then she had to admit, she was really falling for him. In fact, she really had to admit that she had been interested in having Jason for herself since the first time she ever laid eyes on him. And that was before she even knew that Neil liked him.

So what was she doing, letting him go so easily just for the sake of her friendship with Neil? Then it hit her. That was exactly what she was doing: letting Jason go for the sake of her friendship with Neil. After all, she had no choice.

No guy was more important to Jessica than her friendship with Neil. Even if Jason did happen to be straight (which, of course, she knew he was) and even if he was totally in love with her (which wasn't quite as self-evident), she'd still be willing to let him go if it meant saving the special closeness she shared with Neil.

She had never had a friend like Neil before. Someone who accepted her so unapologetically and appreciatively for who she was. Someone who was always there for her, to support her whenever she needed it. And someone who wasn't afraid to ask for her support whenever he needed it.

Jessica had never even felt this close to any of her girlfriends. With Neil there was never any sense of competition and never any of the silly, petty jealousies that she had always experienced at one point or another with the girlfriends she had while she was growing up. Never, she realized, until now.

Yes, it was too late. Jason had already come between them.

But that didn't mean their friendship was necessarily doomed. All Jessica really had to do was keep her word to Neil. To leave Jason alone and let Neil chase him to his heart's content. After all, he'd have to find out sooner or later (and judging from her most recent conversation with him, it looked like it would be sooner) that Jason wasn't gay. And Jessica figured that after that happened, most of the pressure would be off.

She and Neil could go back to being pals again, and once the whole Neil-Jason misunderstanding blew over, she could ease back into pursuing Jason herself. Maybe.

But in the meantime she really did owe it to her best friend to keep her word and stay away from Jason. Which, unfortunately, meant canceling her plans with him for tomorrow. And she had to do it in a way that told him she wouldn't be rescheduling anytime soon. She didn't want to do it on the phone. And she wanted to do it before Jason saw Neil this afternoon.

She really did want to give Neil the chance to make a connection with Jason. And she didn't think that it would be possible—provided that Jason *was* gay, which of course she knew he wasn't—if Jason in any way thought he had to choose between Neil and Jessica. So she had to see Jason. And soon.

Jessica knew that Neil was planning to go to Jason's place in about an hour, so she didn't have much time. Not that she needed much. All she had to do was go over there and tell Jason that she had met someone else, and even though she really liked him, she thought it best that they stop seeing each other.

It would be easy, right? But what if Jason wanted to stay friends with her? Well, she'd just have to tell him that she didn't think that was such a good idea. And what if he told her that he couldn't live without her? That they belonged together and he refused to let her go?

Of course, she doubted very much that he'd say anything of the sort. But it was still fun to flatter herself.

In any event, she had to move fast. She'd just stop by Jason's room and give him the bad news, and then he'd be all Neil's. That is, until Neil found out the truth.

Chapter
Eight

Elizabeth pulled the covers back up over her head. No, she didn't feel quite ready to face the light just yet. Since returning home yesterday from the Sweet Valley Resort Hotel—the very place where her search for Sam had come to such a bizarre ending—she had barely emerged from the warm cocoon of her big, white bed.

At least here she was safe. All alone. With no one around to lie to her.

That's all the outside world was made of. Lies. Suddenly nothing in her life was true. Not even the guy she thought she loved. The guy she had thought was made for her. Now she didn't even know who he was.

Sam Burgess, a fraud. How could she have known? And now she knew nothing.

Who pretends they're someone poor and lazy?

Elizabeth had always thought impostors pretended to be someone above them on the social scale. Like Matt Damon in *The Talented Mr. Ripley*. Or Melanie Griffith in *Working Girl*. So why would a rich kid from Boston pretend to be some broke slacker?

So why? Why him? Why *her*?

There were so many questions swimming around in Elizabeth's head. And she didn't have answers for any of them. Yesterday she didn't know where Sam was. Today she didn't know *who* he was.

It was so ironic. The person who exposed Finn Robinson as a liar turned out to be an even bigger phony himself. Elizabeth tried to strike from her mind all the comparisons she had made between Finn and Sam the day before. Finn's lies had been nothing compared to Sam's grand farce.

Finn was just a guy trying to get her to go to bed with him. Sam had insinuated himself into her life— and, she hated to admit, into her heart—by pretending to be some highly principled, intensely honest, cynical yet sincere, moralistic, intimacy-fearing, lazy, smart-ass pain in the neck.

Who would even pick such a combination to impersonate? Elizabeth wondered what parts of Sam, if any, were really real. She guessed that most of the bad parts were true.

Sam's annoying contentiousness—you just

couldn't fake something like that. The cynicism was genuine too. But his honesty and sincerity—those had to be as fake as a plastic fern. His fear of intimacy was no doubt real, and she was sure he was truly lazy too.

But what bothered her even more than not knowing what parts of Sam were authentic was her realization that every moment she had spent with him, everything they shared, every feeling or emotion that sprang from his presence—none of it was real.

Every time she made him laugh, every time she got upset at him for being a jerk, every time that half of her wanted to kiss him while the other half wanted to strangle him, every insight he made about her character, every time she thought she figured something out about him. Her anxiety over the Kiss. Her worry when Sam disappeared afterward. The Kiss itself.

It was all fiction. Fantasy. A dream.

And Elizabeth was still dreaming. Still bewildered. She still didn't know who Sam Burgess was. As she lay there under her safe, warm blankets, insulated from the world, she thought about turning her back on the fable of Sam Burgess forever. She wanted to forget he ever existed, if in fact he ever did.

But it wouldn't exactly be easy. He was bound to come back eventually. He couldn't stay in his luxury love nest forever, could he? Maybe he could. Just return to the old life he left behind—if there even was such a thing—or simply create a whole new identity for himself. He evidently had the means.

But no. Elizabeth had the feeling that Sam would come back, and all too soon. And when he did, he'd be living in her house again. Right downstairs. Living his lie.

Or maybe he'd finally come clean after all. But even if he did own up to who he really was, Elizabeth knew there would always be more lies. More lies to cover up whatever shreds of his past or present he felt were too dangerous, or too precious, to reveal. She'd never be able to trust him again. That much she did know. And without trust, of course there could never be love.

Elizabeth just wished that she could somehow get to the truth. And without relying on Sam Burgess to bring her there. She knew she would never truly be able to forget him as long as this mystery remained. Yet how could she find out anything true about him if Sam was the only one with the answers? She wondered if he even knew himself who he was. Well, whatever his version of his true self might be, she was sure that it was riddled with lies too.

If only she could find the truth on her own. But

how? Elizabeth wondered if there was anything in Sam's room that might give her clues to his actual identity. But she couldn't go snooping around in his private effects. Even when she had been waiting up for him in his room the other night, the thought of going through his things had never occurred to her. And she wasn't about to violate a housemate's privacy now.

But why not? Why shouldn't she look through his drawers and search his hard drive? Snooping around in Sam's room would be nothing compared to the violation he had perpetrated on Elizabeth. And on Jessica and Neil too. They had bought his story just as much as she had. A poor kid from Boston, who needed a cheap room while he attended Orange County College.

Elizabeth wondered if he even went to OCC. She wondered if Floyd and Bugsy even existed. Of course she knew that Anna was real. That became all too clear at the hotel room yesterday. *"Who's at the door, honey?"* she mimicked silently. *Make me sick!*

Elizabeth thought back to the first time she met Anna. She had always assumed that she was just a girl Sam had met at school. She could tell Anna had a huge crush on him, and Elizabeth figured that Sam had merely used her as a one-night stand. But now it turned out that their connection went deeper. Or did it?

Maybe it was just a coincidence that Elizabeth walked in on Sam and Anna again. Maybe it was really only the second night they spent together. Or maybe they had been sleeping together the whole time. Maybe the entire one-night-stand thing was just part of the act too. Or maybe they hadn't even been sleeping together at the hotel at all. *Yeah, right,* Elizabeth thought. *I wish.*

Wait a second. Why did she even care if Sam was sleeping with Anna? For all Elizabeth cared, Anna could have Sam—whoever he was. But even if she had stopped caring, she couldn't help wondering that very same question. Who was he?

Elizabeth threw the covers off her head and sat straight up in bed. She had had enough solitude. Now she wanted some answers. Her thoughts turned back to Sam's bedroom. Maybe there *were* some clues to be found there. Or maybe not. But either way, she had to do something. She couldn't just stay in bed forever. And she couldn't rely on Sam for any honest answers. Besides, she didn't think she had the stomach to ask him any more questions anyway.

Jessica was just catching her breath by the time she got to Jason's dorm. She had run all the way to campus from the duplex but started walking once she reached the entrance. She didn't mind being slightly flushed when she arrived. But she certainly didn't want to be all sweaty.

She was starting to enjoy her new fitness-minded persona, she mused as she checked her reflection in the door to Jason's building. Especially now that Donna Karan was making workout clothes.

And Jessica had to admit, she was in better shape now than she had been for a very long time. Too bad she was here to break things off with Jason. Dating him might be good for her health.

The door to Jason's room was ajar, so Jessica knocked lightly, not wanting to just barge in without warning. She figured the door would be shut if he wanted privacy, but still, she didn't want to catch him in any compromising position. She hadn't thought until now that she should have called before coming over. What would she say if he had company?

Much to Jessica's satisfaction, Jason was alone when he pulled open his door. Alone and gorgeous.

"Jessica!" Jason sounded surprised, but pleasantly.

"Hey, Jason," Jessica greeted him casually, leaning forward on her toes to peck his cheek. Jason kissed the air beside her ear.

He gestured for her to come inside but left the door open. "So, what brings you to my doorstep?"

"Oh, I was just in the neighborhood," Jessica replied coyly.

"Well, it's good to see you." Jason shoved his hands into the pockets of his khaki cargo pants and then pulled them out to gesture toward the bed. "Do you wanna sit down?"

"No, that's okay. I probably shouldn't stay long anyway." Jessica marveled at the spartan simplicity and sophistication of his room. He had only the bare essentials—desk, chair, computer, bookshelf, stereo, minifridge, and, of course, bed—but everything was so tastefully arranged and appointed. It was also the tidiest guy's room she had ever seen.

"So, what are you up to? Were you out for a run or something?" Jason tried to make small talk while Jessica looked around his room.

Yeah, I'm out for a run, Jessica thought. *I just ran over here to tell you I never want to see you again so that when my gay housemate comes over and starts making moves on you, you won't be thinking about me. Oh, yeah, and then you and Neil can fall in love and live happily ever after.*

Jessica wasn't quite ready to launch into breakup mode, especially with a guy she had never even kissed. What was she even thinking anyway? You didn't exactly tell someone you didn't want to see them again when you weren't even "seeing each

120

other" in the first place. And who had to show up in person to cancel movie plans?

"Um, I was just on campus, visiting a friend who lives in Reid," Jessica lied. "So I thought I'd stop by."

"Well, I'm glad you did."

Jessica stood across from Jason and peered into his gorgeous eyes. "Yeah, I'm glad I did too."

"So, how's your friend Chloe doing?" Jason asked.

"Chloe?" For a moment Jessica was puzzled, but then she recalled that she and Jason had run into Chloe at Yum-Yum's. "Oh, Chloe. She's okay, I guess. Wow, you've got a good memory."

"So has she come to terms with her friend?" he asked, a sly grin forming at the edges of his lips. "What was his name? Martin?"

"Right. Martin." Jessica was genuinely impressed with Jason's faculty for names. "Yeah, I saw them yesterday, and they were still acting a little weird. It's like, they're a couple, but only Martin knows it."

"That's how it seemed to me too." Jason smiled and took a small step toward Jessica. He smelled good, like lavender mingling with a faint smell of citrus. She moved slightly closer to enjoy the scent.

"It's funny how people hook up with each other." Jessica was talking about Chloe and Martin but thinking of her and Jason. "Sometimes it just takes a while for both people to realize that they belong together."

"And all too often they never do," Jason added. Jessica got the sense that he was talking about her and Jason, too. And she could feel the energy between them intensifying.

She tried to remember why she was here. She knew in the back of her mind that she had come here to create distance between her and Jason. But there was a magnetic force that was pulling her inevitably closer to him. It was too powerful to resist.

"So do you think Chloe's ready to let Martin put his arm around her in public?" Jason asked suggestively, inching ever closer to Jessica.

"Are you ready for me to put my arms around you?" Jessica responded, resting her hands gently on his hips.

"I think I am," Jason purred. He moved his lips to meet Jessica's as she moved her hands up his sinewy back, caressing the muscular contours through the ribbed cotton of his black T-shirt.

Jason replaced a lock of Jessica's hair behind her ear and let his fingers linger at the side of her neck as his lips parted around her mouth and his warm breath tickled her tongue.

Her lips reacted by drawing Jason's supple

tongue into her mouth, painting circles around its tip with her own dainty tongue. The mingling of their taste buds was utterly delicious.

Jessica's skin was electrified wherever Jason touched her. From her neck to her shoulders and all the way down to the small of her back, where he allowed his thumb to slide along her waistline. Their tongues did the tango, and Jessica was all but lost in the moment.

She didn't know where she was or why she was here. She was only happy. Jason's breathing got louder, and so did Jessica's, until their disparate breaths formed a percussive harmony all their own. Jessica was lost in this dialogue that involved no words.

But then another voice intruded on the moment. It was neither hers nor Jason's, yet it seemed to be coming from within the room. And when she finally located it in the doorway, the voice was all too familiar.

"If I wasn't seeing this with my own eyes, I wouldn't believe it."

Jessica opened her eyes to see Neil, standing in the doorway and looking like he had just been punched. She and Jason let out synchronized gasps as Neil shook his head and turned to retreat.

Jessica's passion immediately turned to dread. She wanted to go after Neil, but she couldn't quite let go of Jason. The magnetic force was still in effect, yet fading. Jessica gulped, and Jason pursed his lips, tilting his head uncertainly. Both of them dropped their arms to their sides. Jason shrugged and glanced toward the door.

"I guess I should go find Neil," Jessica said at last. "I'm afraid this is kind of complicated."

Jason sighed. "You're telling me."

Jessica rushed out of the room and looked down the hall for Neil. But too much time had already passed. She sprinted for the elevator but got to it just as the doors were closing. Jessica glanced at the stairwell. The last thing she wanted to do was run down twelve flights of steps, but she guessed she didn't have a choice.

By the time she made it to the bottom, she was out of breath and officially sweaty. She burst through the metal door and into the lobby, looking toward the elevator to see if it had arrived ahead of her. The number 2 was lit up above the closed door. Jessica couldn't believe it: She had actually beaten the elevator down. Now she could catch Neil before he left the building and explain what had just happened in Jason's room. *Great.*

But no sooner had Jessica congratulated herself on winning the race against the elevator than the illuminated number changed to 3 instead of 1—the elevator had evidently come all the way down and started up again. She looked around the lobby, but there was no sign of Neil. Jessica ran outside and into the sunlight, but Neil was nowhere to be seen.

Jessica walked dejectedly back inside the dorm building and solemnly rode the elevator back to Jason's floor. But when she returned to his room, the door was closed. She knocked, but no one answered. Jason had disappeared—into thin air, just like Neil.

Oh, well, at least now Jessica didn't have to talk to either of them. Not yet anyway.

Nina sat alone on her bed, her back to the headboard, her knees drawn up to make a little desk out of her legs under her blanket. A physics book lay open, propped up on her knees, and she was dreamily reading the same sentence over and over. *Heisenberg's uncertainty principle reveals the extent to which the measurements of a particle's position and its momentum are mutually exclusive.* It didn't make a lot of sense to her, but it seemed to say that even in science, there are some things you just can't know. Or maybe that some things just aren't out there to be known. She couldn't tell which. It was uncertain. That seemed appropriate. She was uncertain about a lot of things.

Like Josh, for one. Her feelings had been going back and forth on him so much! When she was with him, he could be so great, making her feel secure and happy, or he could be a jerk. And sometimes she couldn't tell which. Then when she was alone, it just got worse. If she let herself, she could imagine them together in a serious way, in the kind of real, committed relationship she wanted. But she had to draw herself up short, to tell herself not to get her hopes up unreasonably. She would try to remember that they'd been together only a couple of times and that she wasn't really in a position to know whether he was feeling like that about her—and that maybe he didn't know how he felt on his own part. Was it just that she couldn't discern his feelings or that there wasn't enough there to discern? There was no way to tell.

Her pencil traced over doodles in the margins. She wished she could have a sign, some magical way to tell her which way to go. *You're being silly,* she told herself. *You've got nothing to do but to wait.* But that wasn't the answer she wanted to hear, and soon she found her mind wandering again over the different possibilities.

When she had wanted just to get out of his room that morning, he had lured her back into bed with his gentle caresses. After they had made love a second time, though, he had been quiet when she wanted to talk and had eventually fallen asleep in the middle of their conversation. Still feeling affectionate toward him, she had dressed silently, left him a little note, and crept out of his room.

As the day had passed, though, doubts had begun to gnaw at her again. Sure, he had been a darling toward her in the birdsong hour—but he had woken up with one thing on his mind, hadn't he? It did seem that his sweet moods coincided pretty directly with his carnal desires. And when he was satisfied, he would drift away from her, just when she was feeling closest.

Nina's empirical mind tallied up the cases, and she couldn't help but draw the conclusion that he might just be nice when he wanted sex. Or maybe it was just the way it happened to have worked out the few times they'd been together. She knew that to have any better certainty, she'd need to run a lot more "experiments." But these weren't sterile lab routines; this was risking her own heart. She couldn't be objective—the conditions necessary for her to gain certainty required her to persist in the course of which she was so unsure. There was no way to be certain beforehand. Arrgh!

Nina resolved to put it out of her mind until she'd had more time to mull it over. Maybe if she could sleep on it. But first she had to finish her reading. Her course work was the one thing that she *could* control, and she steeled herself to do just that and began to dissect the equations on the page in front of her. After a minute or two she was deep in concentration, and her own situation was far away. And then the phone rang.

"Hello?" she said.

It was Josh. "Hi, Nina!"

"Oh, hi, Josh! I was just thinking about you," she fibbed.

"Uh-oh! Anything good?"

"Yeah," she cooed. "Lots of good things."

"Well, I must have been thinking about you at the same time. Good things. That's why I called."

"So, how was your Tuesday?"

"I had a lab in chemistry that took all afternoon. We couldn't seem to get the apparatus to work right. It was pretty frustrating."

"Yeah," Nina said. "I hate that."

"But you and I seemed to have *our* chemistry working pretty well this morning!" he flirted.

Nina blushed. "It did work pretty well, didn't it?"

"Very well, I'd say. I wished you'd stayed awhile. I was sad to see you weren't there when I woke up."

"Oh, I wanted to stay," Nina assured him. "But you know how it is. Morning lecture. I thought I'd better let you sleep. And I had to get breakfast before class." That wasn't really the whole truth, but it wasn't false either. Really she had mostly wanted to get out of his room while she was still feeling happy about him.

"That was nice of you. Especially after you kept me up so late last night."

"I kept *you* up?" she teased. "You kept *me* up."

"I guess we kept each other up."

"Yeah," she said, and they were quiet for a while.

"I had a really nice time," Josh said.

"Yeah, me too," Nina said. She felt awkward. She couldn't ask him what she was thinking: Did you have a good time because we had sex, or did you want to have sex because we were having a good time? That was *not* a question you were allowed to ask. The silence between them grew.

Josh said, "So, how's your work going, Miss Summa Cum Laude?"

"Oh, c'mon, Josh." She giggled. "We've both got a long way to go. But it's going all right, I guess. I'm kind of worried about English, really. There's a lot I'm not getting in *The Sun Also Rises*."

"Aww, I don't see how they even grade those classes," Josh scoffed. "It's all just a matter of opinion."

Nina paused. She wasn't so sure about it. It did seem that some of the other students had much more interesting things to say than she did. But she didn't want to disagree with Josh. "Well, they do grade you, and it does count for your average."

"If you're pretty much caught up, would you like to go to the movies with me tomorrow night?

They're showing something in the student-center auditorium that looks cool: *The Man Who Knew Too Much*. Hitchcock. Eee! Eee! Eee! Eee!" Josh made the scary sounds from *Psycho*.

Nina was delighted. He was asking her out again, and when they went to the movie together, they could be seen in front of all the other students who were there. This was much better than sneaking out of the library for a cappuccino that turned into sex. Maybe her friends would be there too. Maybe this meant he was going to be her boyfriend.

"That sounds like fun, Josh," she said coolly. She didn't want to sound too eager. "What time is it playing?"

"Seven and nine-thirty. We could go early and eat after or go late and eat before. Whatever you want."

"Nine o'clock's a little late to eat, don't you think? Why don't we go to the late show?"

"Sounds good to me. There's a new Japanese noodle restaurant in town I've been wanting to try. It looks pretty good, and it's cheap. Whaddaya say?"

"I say, okay!" Nina laughed. "Sounds great."

"All right. Should I come get you in your room at seven?"

"Okay," Nina said. "Seven, it is."

"Okay, then. Good night," Josh said.

"Good night," she repeated.

"Night," he said quickly, and hung up.

Nina hung up the phone with a smile. It did seem like a sign. If they were going to go out together as a couple, though, what was she going to wear? It should be something special. It was time to go shopping. *Definitely* shopping. In which case she was going to have to get finished studying tonight since tomorrow she was going to be busy at the mall. She rubbed her eyes, turned back to her textbook, and concentrated on Dr. Heisenberg and his mysterious principle.

Chapter Nine

Elizabeth crept into Sam's room and slowly closed the door behind her. She could hardly believe she was doing this. Snooping around in hopes of finding some clues about his true identity. She had never done anything so sneaky, and the whole thing just felt wrong. How would she feel if someone were digging through her personal stuff while she was away? She wouldn't like it; that went without saying.

But after the magnificent fraud that Sam had perpetrated on Elizabeth and the entire household, she felt justified in everything she did behind Sam's back. At least she wasn't deceiving him to his face, like he had been doing all along. And once she found out what she needed to, she was perfectly willing to tell Sam what she had done. And where she had been. She knew there was nothing he could really say about a little rummage through his files, especially when his entire existence had been a sham.

She looked around the room and wondered which of Sam's possessions were even real. And which were props. She looked at the giant wall map of Africa in an entirely new light. She had always thought it was strange when Sam spoke of wanting to visit Africa someday. Now she wondered if he hadn't already been there.

She imagined him traveling there on safari with his father every summer. Sam had always claimed to be a pacifist. Now she pictured him leveling a rifle at endangered species and mounting his trophies in the dark-wood library of his family's mansion somewhere.

Elizabeth glanced up at the Ferrari poster and snorted. His "dream car." Yeah, right. He probably had one parked in the garage at home. Wherever that was.

Soon she would know. Soon Elizabeth would know everything. She returned her thoughts to the matter at hand: searching Sam's rooms for clues. She'd start with his desk, looking for any papers that might give her a hint about his real identity or where his family was. If nothing turned up there, then she'd turn on his computer and see what she found there. Maybe there would be some telling e-mails.

Or perhaps she could access his stock portfolio. Sam had always scoffed at anything having to do with money, from gambling to electronic trading. But she bet that in reality he had millions invested in various dot.com companies and assorted hedge funds. His parents probably even owned a casino too.

But as she walked stealthily toward his desk, afraid of making too much noise and drawing Neil or Jessica into the room, Elizabeth started having second thoughts again.

What could she really find out about Sam by sneaking through his stuff anyway? Even if she did find out how much he was really worth, or who his father was, or what other resorts his family owned, would any of it really tell her about who the actual Sam Burgess was?

No. Knowing where a person grew up, or who his parents were, or even how much money they had in the bank—none of this would reveal the true nature of a person. A person's parents or stock portfolio might shed some light on what a person was like or what they could afford. But their real identity could be grasped only through spending time with them. Talking to them and listening.

Elizabeth began to wonder if the Sam she had come to know—or thought she knew anyway— might actually be the genuine person he was.

Maybe his bank account and his family's financial holdings were the only things he lied about after all. And maybe he had good reason to keep those things a secret.

No, Elizabeth couldn't believe that. There was never any good reason to lie to your friends. Whatever the truth was about Sam's background or his family, Elizabeth could have handled it. And anything he might have told her—no matter how horrible—as long as it was true, she would have understood.

And Elizabeth knew that lies, no matter how big or small, always bred more lies. So even if Sam had told lies that he thought were necessary to protect him from whatever ugly truth he felt the need to conceal, he must have told a hundred more lies just to keep his original lies from being revealed.

Elizabeth's head began to spin as she tried to fathom the endless web of deceit that Sam had spun under her very nose. She had to get to the truth. And now.

But first there was another truth she had to face. And that was the honest truth of Elizabeth's own character. Truth and honesty, precisely. Elizabeth Wakefield had always prided herself on being painfully honest. Even when her twin sister was able to effortlessly fib to cover up a mistake or lead a boy to like her, Elizabeth was never able to play along.

Her sense of decency, her sense of self, never allowed it.

Now she felt that Sam's unforgivable deception was leading her to violate her own true character. And no matter how much she rationalized it with examples of Sam's deceit, she could never justify it.

What was she doing here? Violating a housemate's privacy just to get at some morsel of truth? This was ridiculous, especially since she knew that discovering the real Sam Burgess could never be achieved by digging up information behind his back.

As much as she hated the thought of talking to Sam ever again, Elizabeth knew that if she really cared enough to uncover the truth about Sam Burgess, it would be possible only by confronting him face-to-face.

So before she stooped to snoop through any of his drawers or even deigned to turn on his computer, Elizabeth had no choice but to stop herself.

She was still furious. She was still hurting. But lowering herself to Sam's level of deceit was no way to get better. Feeling low for even coming into his room in the first place but big enough to at least resist the temptation to pry, Elizabeth pulled herself away from Sam's secret universe. And dragged her sorry self back upstairs to the sanctuary of her own bedroom.

*   *   *

Neil shut the front door behind him. He leaned back against the door and took a deep breath. Then he exhaled for the first time since leaving Jason's dorm room. Jason's *doorway* was more like it since he hadn't actually gotten the chance to go inside. He supposed he could have hung around. He might have been invited in. That is, if Jessica and Jason ever finished with their little kissy-face exhibition.

But no, Neil thought it best to create as much distance between himself and the new happy couple as humanly possible. Which was why he'd rushed out of the building and come straight home. He guessed he wasn't going to be studying with Jason after all. He wondered if he'd be able to concentrate enough to even study alone for his econ exam. The image of Jason and Jessica sucking face as they groped each other was so vivid in his mind, he wondered if he'd be able to form another mental image as long as he lived.

He knew for sure that he didn't feel like seeing either of their faces in person ever again.

It was still difficult to process what had just occurred. For one thing, what were Jason and Jessica even thinking? They both knew that Neil had plans to pick up Jason at his room. So if they were going to be there making out, they could have at least kept the door closed.

It was almost like they wanted him to catch

them in the throes of passion. Like it was some kind of sick plan to push Neil out of both of their lives. Well, if that's what they were up to, then they had succeeded.

So why had Jessica kept insisting that she was going after Jason to spare Neil the humiliation of finding out the hard way that Jason was straight? Talk about humiliation. Talk about the hard way!

The funny thing was, even after seeing what he saw with his very own eyes, Neil still clung to the belief that Jason was gay. Call it stubbornness, call it stupidity, call it gaydar malfunction. But even while he doubted that *he* would ever have a chance with Jason, Neil also doubted that Jessica would either.

But he couldn't keep spinning these thoughts around inside his own head. He had to talk to someone. He had to get to the bottom of why Jessica would be so eager and willing to violate their friendship like that. Why had she told Neil that Jason was all his if she was going to swoop in at the eleventh hour and try to take him for herself? He knew that she could be conniving, but he also thought that their friendship meant more.

Neil wondered if Elizabeth was still in her room. She had been cooped up in there for almost twenty-four hours. And every time he tried to check on her, she insisted everything was fine and told him to go away. He had figured she was still mad at him for his lack of concern over Sam's supposed disappearance. But he had been so caught up in his drama with Jessica and Jason that he hadn't really put much thought into what Elizabeth was going through.

He knew something strange was going on between her and Sam, but he hadn't quite been able to put his finger on it. Whatever it was, if Elizabeth was still in seclusion, it had to be something serious.

Maybe if he went to her on the pretense of talking about his own problems, she might open up about hers. And even if she didn't, at least he'd be able to get some things off his own chest. And maybe even get some insights into Jessica's behavior from her twin sister.

Neil walked upstairs and knocked gently on Elizabeth's door. No answer. He knocked again, louder, and pressed his ear against the door. She didn't respond, but Neil could swear he heard some rustling inside.

He slowly turned the knob and opened the door just enough to peek his head inside. "Elizabeth?"

"What?" she huffed from beneath the covers. "Just go away."

"Elizabeth?" He spoke softly. "It's me, Neil."

"I know who it is. Just please go away," she pleaded unconvincingly.

Neil thought back on the times when he had

refused to speak about what was on his mind when deep down he was dying to spill his guts. He couldn't help but think that Elizabeth was feeling the same way.

"Elizabeth, I really need to talk to you." Neil could feel authentic desperation creeping into his voice. He realized that he needed to talk to Elizabeth far more than he needed to hear about her problems. "Are you all right?"

Elizabeth poked her head out from beneath her blankets.

"Yes, I'm fine." She groaned.

She didn't look it. Elizabeth's usually perfect blond hair was a tangled mess, like a Barbie doll's that had been stuck at the bottom of the toy chest. She wasn't wearing any makeup, and her vibrant pink skin now looked red and splotchy and especially puffy around her eyes.

Neil realized he must not look much better. Because when Elizabeth took a good look at him, she sounded every bit as concerned for him as he felt about her.

"The question is, are you all right?" Elizabeth sat up in bed and squinted at Neil, as if to more closely inspect his face. "Neil, you look awful."

"Hey, thanks." Neil let out a nervous chuckle. "You know, you don't look so hot yourself."

"Yeah, well . . ." Elizabeth's voice cracked as if

she were on the verge of tears. She gave a dismissive wave of her hand.

Neil could tell that she wasn't ready to talk about whatever was bothering her, so he decided to go first. He figured she could use something to get her mind off whatever was making her so miserable. And if he didn't clear his own conscience of the atrocity he had just witnessed, he was afraid he might explode.

"Elizabeth, something awful just happened."

Elizabeth snapped to attention. She smoothed her hair with her hands and leaned forward. "What is it?"

"Well, you know how Jessica and I have been sort of fighting over the same guy lately?"

Elizabeth nodded in recognition. "Yes. Jason, right?"

"Yeah, well, it's sort of funny because this guy Jason is so obviously gay, and . . ." Neil paused as the image of Jessica and Jason flashed in his mind again.

Elizabeth finished the sentence for him. "And Jessica swears that he's straight."

"Right." Neil took a breath and exhaled. "Well, to make a long story short, I was supposed to go meet Jason to study with him and maybe get a drink afterward. And when I got to his room, Jessica was already there, and they were, like, *intertwined*."

142

"You mean, they were having sex?" Elizabeth was shocked.

"No, no, no, they weren't having sex," Neil quickly clarified. "But they were totally making out. I mean, they both had their clothes on, but they were all over each other. And the crazy thing about it was, Jason's door was literally wide open. So it's not like I barged in on them or anything. It was almost like they were putting on some kind of performance. It was so brazen, so . . . disgusting."

Neil could see Elizabeth's eyes welling up again. But this time he was sure that it was out of sympathy for him.

"Oh my gosh, Neil, I am so sorry," she gushed. "Jeez, I can't believe that happened."

It was strange. Neil suddenly felt so much better, having told someone about what happened. And to get a sympathetic response didn't hurt either. He looked at Elizabeth as she appeared to be trying to think of something more to say. As if she were searching in her own mind for a way to explain her sister's deeds.

"There must be some sort of explanation for this," Elizabeth finally concluded.

"Yeah," Neil jeered. "All's fair in love and war."

"Come on, Neil. Jessica sometimes lacks self-control. But I can't believe she'd actually try to steal someone away from you. You're her best friend."

"Yeah, I *was* her best friend," Neil corrected her. "Or so I thought."

"Listen," Elizabeth started again. She was obviously having trouble getting her mind around what Jessica had done. "Maybe what you said about it being like some kind of performance—maybe there's something to that. Maybe it *was* just an act or something."

"Yeah, maybe they were rehearsing for the school play," Neil scoffed.

"Well, I really don't know what happened," Elizabeth admitted. "But I just think you should keep an open mind about it until you hear Jessica's version of the story."

"I guess you're right." Neil relented. Maybe he was being a little harsh toward Jessica. If their friendship was as strong as both of them had always insisted it was, then he didn't see how he could just forsake it all over one little kiss.

He did feel much better now that he had had this chat with Elizabeth. And he was willing to wait until he spoke to Jessica before he passed any final judgments on her or on Jason, for that matter.

"Thanks, Elizabeth," he concluded. "Thanks for listening."

"Anytime," she answered graciously. "You know where to find me."

"Yeah, speaking of which, I was wondering if

you ever planned on leaving your bedroom again."

The comment seemed to catch Elizabeth off guard, and a smile spread across her face for the first time since Neil had entered her room. "Yeah, eventually," she answered, her smile quickly fading. "When I'm ready."

"Anything you want to talk about?"

"Maybe later." Elizabeth nodded and managed a half smile. "Thanks."

"Well, you know where to find me too. Take care of yourself, okay?" Neil reached down and gave Elizabeth's foot a tender squeeze through the comforter, then turned to leave.

Sam Burgess sat slumped over his beer at Frankie's and pondered his pathetic lie of a life. What did he think he was doing here anyway? Drowning his sorrows?

Of course he knew he wasn't. This was only his first beer, and he probably wouldn't even have another one. But Frankie's had always been a place where he could be alone when he wanted to think. He liked the dim lighting, the smoky atmosphere, and the anonymity of the place. Well, he'd liked the anonymity of the place until he found out that Todd Wilkins worked here.

Now Todd was one of the minor annoyances that Sam was willing to put up with at Frankie's.

Like the four Celine Dion songs on the jukebox or the crummy beer selection. But at least the beer here was cheap, Sam reminded himself. And most of the waitresses were pretty cute too. Besides, Todd wasn't that bad, especially when Sam compared him to Elizabeth's other ex-boyfriends.

And ever since Sam found out that Todd worked at Frankie's, his attitude toward him had mellowed considerably. For the most part Sam still felt his familiar sense of anonymity here. For instance, he knew he'd never see Elizabeth Wakefield at Frankie's.

And even though he felt like a total worm to admit it, she was still the one person he was trying to avoid. Although he could probably add Neil and Jessica to the list now too. Elizabeth had no doubt already told them what a fraud he was. But he wasn't really worried about those two. When they heard his reasons for hiding the truth, he was sure they'd understand. But where Elizabeth was concerned, he wasn't so certain.

"Hey, Sam, what's happening?" Todd Wilkins suddenly appeared behind the bar and extended his hand to shake.

"What's up, Todd." Sam pronounced it more as a statement than a question. He certainly didn't want an answer. Shaking hands with Todd was more than enough social interaction for Sam tonight.

"So what's going on, buddy?" Todd was still facing Sam from behind the bar. He looked rip-roarin' ready for some small talk.

Sam tried to sound as unenthusiastic as possible. "Not much. Just sitting here with my beer."

"Alone with your thoughts, eh?" Todd said cheerfully.

"Yep, until you came along," Sam answered matter-of-factly.

"Oh, I get it. You *want* to be alone." Todd's voice was more sour than understanding.

"Yeah, man." Sam tried to soften his tone. "I'm sorry. I've just got a lot on my mind right now."

"That's cool. I understand."

"Well, I hope you're not going to be standing *right there* the whole night," Sam answered, completely deadpan.

Todd look startled for a moment, then broke into a huge grin. He walked away, shaking his head. "You're a funny guy, you know that, Sam?"

Yeah, real funny, Sam thought. *Try telling that to Elizabeth. Or Anna, for that matter.*

It was beginning to sink in for Sam that he had now alienated the two girls he truly cared about in this world. And talking to Todd Wilkins wasn't going to help him any either. To think, he had called Anna for advice about how to deal with Elizabeth, and then she ended up hating him too.

147

Oh, well. It wasn't all that bad, he told himself. Sam was sure he could work things out with Anna. She was just a friend. But Elizabeth was so much more. Or so he had once thought. Now he'd be lucky if she ever allowed him to speak to her again. It was funny. For the past few days, talking to Elizabeth was the one thing in the world he wanted to avoid. And now he was afraid he'd never get the chance to tell her how he really felt about her.

He thought about everything Anna had told him. Or rather, everything *he* had told *her*. When he looked back on their conversation at the hotel, he had really done most of the talking. Anna just validated what he had to say.

And what, exactly, had he said? That he should just tell her the truth? Unfortunately, ever since Elizabeth walked in on them at the hotel, he had a whole lot more truth to explain. Not just how he felt about her, but who he was and why he had lied about his past. It was all so much more complicated now. He guessed he'd just have to take it one step at a time.

He'd tell her the truth. That the only thing he knew for sure was that he wanted her. He didn't know what that meant, where it would lead. He just knew he wanted to be with her.

That was the truth.

And he *could* imagine himself actually saying all

that. But that had been before Elizabeth had seen him with Anna in the hotel he owned.

Because his less than authentic identity was a whole other matter to deal with now. Sam didn't have any problem with who he was as a person. And he always felt comfortable presenting himself as he truly believed he was. The only thing he'd really lied about was his family. But he couldn't expect Elizabeth to understand that or, for that matter, even believe it.

But he had to give her the chance.

You have to level with her once and for all, Sam told himself. *Not only about how you feel for her, but who you really are. You have to tell her everything: about Mom and Dad and the whole family, why you have to keep their wealth a secret, and why you refuse to spend their money.*

But if he told her all that, then she'd know everything about him. And no doubt she'd try to change him. Sam could just imagine Elizabeth attempting to mold him into some kind of responsible adult with a purpose in life. Why couldn't he just be himself, without everyone knowing everything about him? Why did love have to be such a drag?

Chapter
Ten

Elizabeth's talk with Neil somehow made her feel better. Even though she hadn't felt ready to discuss everything that was going on with Sam, she was relieved to hear that her love life wasn't the only one that was in shambles. Elizabeth didn't want anyone else to suffer, of course, least of all her friend Neil or her twin sister, but at least it was nice to know that she wasn't alone in her confusion. Maybe it was something in the air.

But now she really did feel ready to talk. Maybe not to Neil, though. He might not be as shocked as Elizabeth had been to find out that someone had been keeping a part of his life a secret. But she had to tell *someone* about what happened at the hotel— *Nina,* of course! She had to talk to Nina. But something made Elizabeth pause. She remembered her brief conversation with Nina from yesterday. Elizabeth had been too distracted by her search for Sam to really pay attention to what Nina had been saying to her. It had had something to do with some guy she might be going out with, but that was all Elizabeth could remember. Darn it!

Reviewing the conversation in her mind and realizing how little of it she could recall, Elizabeth felt guilty. Nina was always there for her, and Elizabeth was always ready to reach out for her loyal and patient ear, but when Nina had had something to talk with Elizabeth about—something that Elizabeth ought to be able to help her with—Elizabeth had been too wrapped up in her confusion over Sam to even listen to her with the attention she deserved. Elizabeth couldn't even remember the guy's name.

Well, it wasn't too late to remedy that! She'd call Nina up and get the lowdown on the whole situation. How complicated could it be? Nina was pretty inexperienced with guys, and Elizabeth was pretty sure that she could figure out what was going on in a jiffy and give her the Wakefield diagnosis.

And then she could share her revelation about Sam. Elizabeth was sure Nina would be more than interested to hear that Sam's parents secretly owned the Sweet Valley Resort Hotel. Or rather that Sam was the secret son of the owners of the hotel. And maybe down-to-earth Nina's reaction could give

Elizabeth a clue about how she might really feel inside about it herself. An external perspective, an objective view. Nina, her best friend, her pocket scientist. How handy! She dialed Nina's number, hoping she could catch her in her room.

She was in luck. "Hello?" Nina's voice sounded happy.

"Nina, hey!" Elizabeth sang.

The line was quiet for a moment. "Elizabeth?" Nina asked, sounding surprised.

"Yeah, hey, it's me. What's up?"

Nina paused again. She coughed and then said nothing, as if the question had taken her by surprise. "Oh, I was just studying," she said. She sounded distant, almost defensive, as if she were trying to hide something. But she didn't say anything more.

Elizabeth felt a pang of guilty panic as the idea began to occur to her that Nina had been hurt more by their conversation than she might have realized.

"Listen, Nina," she offered, "I'm sorry I was so short with you yesterday on the phone. Things have been a little crazy around here for a while. But I wanted to hear what your deal was with this *new guy*." She sounded a little phony even to her own ear, but that was the lead Nina should have taken up to talk about him. Still nothing but silence.

Elizabeth tried again. "Wasn't there something you wanted to ask me about him?"

Nina was quiet for a second. "Well," she said quietly, "that's okay. I think I've pretty much got it figured out. Yeah, I'm okay on everything. Thanks, though." She sounded perfunctory, as if she were turning down a magazine subscription.

"No problem, Nina," Elizabeth answered, trying to sound enthusiastic. "Are you sure you don't want to talk about it?"

Nina's voice was a little condescending. "Yeah, I'm pretty sure," she answered evenly.

"What's his name again?"

"Josh."

"Um, so what's he like?"

"I don't know, really. Smart, I guess."

"Just like you, hmmm? What's he studying, brain surgery?" Elizabeth winced to herself. She knew she sounded stupid. But Nina wasn't giving her an opening!

"Uh, no. Engineering. He's an engineering major."

Elizabeth had nothing to say about engineering. "Oh," she offered lamely. "That's cool."

Somehow Elizabeth wasn't very excited anymore about talking to her best friend. She felt like she was prying as she tried to draw Nina out. On the other hand, she thought, maybe Nina really just didn't feel like talking about it. Elizabeth could

154

understand that. Maybe Nina was too nervous about it and not really mad at her at all. But Elizabeth had kept the news about Sam inside her for so long, she was afraid she'd burst if she didn't tell someone about it soon. She thought she'd try Nina out on that front.

"Listen, Nina? He sounds great. You'll have to bring him by the duplex. But look, there is something I've been *dying* to tell you. You will not believe what a phony Sam Burgess has turned out to be. All this time we had no idea—"

"Oh, actually, Elizabeth, this really isn't the best time," Nina answered curtly, cutting her off. "I've really got to get back to my work. It's kind of hard, and I want to figure it out before I go to sleep. It's kind of late."

Elizabeth couldn't miss the pointedness of her reply. She tried another approach, a sort of motherly tone that she'd had to take with Nina in the past.

"Nina, listen," Elizabeth said knowingly. "If you're mad at me about the way I treated you yesterday, I understand. It was really unfair. Things are really weird around here—you won't believe what I just found out about Sam—and, well, I'm sorry if I was sort of out to lunch. I was just in a bad space, you know? But you don't have to be short with me just to get me back. I wasn't trying to hurt you."

She regretted saying it as soon as it came out of her mouth. She hadn't meant to impute such small motives to Nina.

After a long pause Nina responded calmly, "Elizabeth, I don't know what you're talking about. I'm not mad at you!" Her voice was sickly sweet. In fact, it sounded to Elizabeth the way she sometimes sounded when talking to her own mother. "The truth is, I have a huge test I need to study for right now, and it's really just not the best time for me to be talking to you. I'm sorry if it makes you upset, but you know I need to do well in school, and I just can't gossip about guys right now."

Elizabeth couldn't believe her ears. She felt stung. What was Nina's problem anyway? Well, whatever it was, she obviously didn't have time for Elizabeth now, so there was no point in keeping her on the phone. She was going to have some patching up to do, but it wasn't the top item on her list of priorities. She *had* to tell someone about Sam, and if Nina was going to be huffy, she was going to have to find somebody else.

"Okay," she answered uncertainly. "I understand. I'm being shallow, right? Well, that's me, Elizabeth the social butterfly. I guess I'd better let you get back to the old books."

"Right, Elizabeth, the stupid old books. Nina the bookworm." Nina's voice was saccharine—or was she being self-deprecating? Elizabeth couldn't tell. "So, I'll see you around, okay?"

"Okay," Elizabeth said. "See you around." She paused, waiting to see if Nina would take the opportunity to soften things between them a little. But she didn't. She just said good night, and when Elizabeth said good night back, Nina hung up.

Elizabeth set the phone down in a daze. She couldn't believe what had just happened. Her best friend didn't have time to talk to her because she had to study? It was bizarre. How mad could she be? Maybe it wasn't just the conversation from before. Maybe Nina really was looking down on Elizabeth for not being as serious as Nina about school. Elizabeth had never before thought that she would be snubbed by Nina! She felt completely confused and pretty hurt too. *I guess Nina's really changing,* she thought. *And maybe not in such a good way. Not for the better anyway.*

Nina hung up the phone, a pang of guilt worrying her in a little spot between her eyes. She knew she had been rude to Elizabeth, hurtful even, and she hadn't really wanted to be. She wasn't mad at Elizabeth anymore for being unsupportive about her problems with Josh, but on the other hand, she hadn't really wanted to talk with her about him. It was kind of just too late. She had needed a friend to talk with about Josh before she slept with him, not after, and now it would be too complicated to try to explain everything. Not just too complicated to explain, but even to understand herself. She would rather just let the chips fall where they may. She knew what she was doing, she decided.

And then there would have been the problem of trying to explain to Elizabeth how she had felt when Elizabeth had blown her off on the phone. She wanted to let Elizabeth know that she had been hurt, but she still didn't want to get into it right now.

Nina knew it wasn't going to be easy. Elizabeth was such a perfectionist—if Nina had said that Elizabeth had done something wrong, Elizabeth would go to any lengths to convince herself that it hadn't really been her fault. That was just her way. And somehow, whenever Nina had tried to make a little space for herself in their relationship in the past, Elizabeth had always made it seem that it was she, Nina, who was being demanding and overbearing, whereas Nina knew perfectly well that most of the time their relationship was really more about Elizabeth. Nina had an important role to play, but everyone knew that Elizabeth was the star. And Nina didn't mind that really, not in the big picture.

But it could go too far, and Elizabeth's being so obsessed with Sam to the point that she couldn't even listen to Nina talk about her crisis with Josh was taking it too far. Nina recalled how sad and alone she had felt in the library, and the cold feeling inside her made her huddle up with her blanket. *Just you, girl,* she said to herself. *Just me, myself, and I.*

And besides, Nina thought. What was all that business with Sam? Who *cared*? Nina couldn't understand why Elizabeth would get so wrapped up in him. It was bad enough to get ignored by her best friend, but over Sam Burgess? Something was definitely wrong with Elizabeth. *Or maybe she's really changing,* Nina thought. *Maybe we're both changing. But Elizabeth's changes are definitely* not *for the better.*

Elizabeth was waiting for her sister to get home. After her less than satisfying chat with Nina, she couldn't wait to spill the beans about Sam to Jessica. After her talk with Neil she realized that she couldn't just keep her confusion over Sam bottled up inside her.

As soon as she heard Jessica come in the door, Elizabeth jumped from the couch and ran to meet her before she had a chance to go upstairs. "Jessica, you'll never guess what I found out about Sam!"

Jessica was hardly intrigued. "What? He's actually a serial killer, and he finally got arrested?"

Elizabeth frowned. "Jessica, that's not even funny."

"I'm sorry, Elizabeth," Jessica answered tiredly. "But I'm not feeling very funny right now."

"Well, don't you want to hear about what I found out?" Elizabeth pressed her.

"Okay, what is it this time?" Jessica asked with a heavy sigh.

Elizabeth was beginning to wonder what was wrong with the world. Or at least with *her* world. First she found the one true thing in her life shacked up in a luxury hotel with another girl and discovered that he'd been hiding a secret identity for the entire time she'd known him. And then her best friend and her own sister weren't even interested in hearing about it.

Well, she wasn't going to wait any longer. Jessica was just going to have to listen to her, whether she wanted to or not.

"Remember how Sam's been missing for the past few days?" Elizabeth began.

Jessica nodded like she was listening to a broken record. "Uh-huh."

"Well, guess where he's been?" she asked excitedly.

"Why don't you tell me," Jessica replied flatly.

"He was at the Sweet Valley Resort Hotel, and he was with that Anna girl, and get this, they were staying in the owner's suite." Elizabeth's heart began to race as she recounted the story.

"The owner's suite?" Jessica repeated. "What was he doing in the owner's suite?"

160

"I thought you'd never ask." Elizabeth took a deep breath and exhaled. "The reason he was in the owner's suite is because his family owns the hotel!"

"What?" Jessica was perplexed. "But that's impossible. His dad's a, um, I don't know, something that doesn't make a lot of money, though."

"Yes, that's what he's been telling us all along," Elizabeth explained anxiously. "That he's some blue-collar kid from Boston. But the truth is that he's really some rich kid, and his parents own the Sweet Valley Resort Hotel."

"That's so weird," Jessica replied thoughtfully. "So, Sam's been living a lie this whole time?"

"It looks that way." Elizabeth stared down at the floor, her eyes beginning to well with tears.

Jessica looked at Elizabeth with a look of genuine concern. "So where do you fit into all of this?"

"That's just it," Elizabeth answered, her voice barely a croak. "I really have no idea. I mean, the last time I saw you, I was going out to look for him to tell him I wanted to give this thing between us a try, whatever it was. And then when I finally found him, not only was he with some other girl, but now he's not even the same guy I thought I might be in love with."

"Oh God, that's awful." Jessica stepped toward Elizabeth and put her hand on her shoulder. "What are you going to do?"

161

Now that Elizabeth was finally getting some support, now that she finally felt safe, here with her twin sister, someone who she absolutely knew was real—and who she knew would always be there for her—it was like it was finally okay to break down. To release all the pent-up emotion she had been keeping inside herself.

"That's just it, Jess," she sobbed. "I don't know what to do."

Jessica pulled her sister closer and put her arms around Elizabeth. "Everything's going to be okay, Elizabeth. You're going to be fine, I promise."

"But you don't understand," Elizabeth blurted out amidst the tears. "Everything we shared, every moment Sam and I spent together, it was all a lie. And I . . . I was such a fool. I was such a fool!"

"Let it out, Elizabeth," Jessica urged her. "I'm here for you now. I'm listening; just let it out."

All of a sudden Elizabeth could feel the energy shift in the living room. She knew even before she heard his voice that Neil had come downstairs.

"Oh, please," he shouted sarcastically. "I'm surprised you can even relate, Jessica. Especially since you're Ms. Betrayal herself!"

"Neil, this isn't the time, okay?" Jessica called up.

Elizabeth looked up from Jessica's shoulder to

see Neil eyeing her and then Jessica and then glancing at Elizabeth again. He glared at Jessica and then turned to go back upstairs in a huff. She was grateful to Jessica for not following him upstairs. The drama with Jason could wait. Right now Elizabeth needed her sister.

Chapter
Eleven

It was long after midnight by the time Sam returned home. The glow of the television greeted him when he walked in the door. Neil's greeting wasn't so pleasant.

"So, dude, it looks like you're busted," Neil remarked, without turning around to face Sam. He could feel the icy disregard emanating from the back of Neil's head.

Sam knew immediately that the jig was up. And he felt like a total jerk. Not only had he managed to turn Anna and Elizabeth against him, but now Jessica and Neil probably hated him too.

And Sam had always liked them both. But it didn't matter. He had lied to them. Not that he had any choice. There was no way he could have told them how rich his family was and still have been able to live his life the way he wanted to. There's no way they would have let him get away with it. There would have been too many expectations, too many questions. They probably wouldn't have even let him move in in the first place if they knew he could afford to pay rent for the entire duplex himself.

But the real truth, Sam told himself, was that he *couldn't* afford that. Since he refused to spend any of his parents' money, he really did need a cheap place to live.

But here was Neil. No rich parents, no luxury hotel he could stop into when he needed to get away. He even relied on student loans for his college education. If anyone needed a cheap room in a duplex like this, it was Neil. And all along he had probably thought that Sam was just like him.

Well, now he knew that Sam had been lying about his past all along. And Sam didn't expect to be forgiven.

He only hoped he could make them understand—Neil and Jessica as well as Elizabeth. But if Neil's present attitude was any indication, it didn't seem too likely.

Sam walked quietly to the big easy chair beside the couch that faced the television. He lowered himself slowly into the chair so as not to disturb Neil's late night viewing and waited until there was a commercial before he spoke. "So, I guess you heard."

"Yep," Neil answered without taking his eyes from the TV.

He certainly wasn't making it easy on Sam. But then again, why should he? Sam had lied to him. He'd lied to everyone. Neil, Jessica, and Elizabeth had welcomed him into their home, and he had never had the decency to tell them who he really was. Not that he had lied in order to get the room. Not really anyway.

Sam was already living his clandestine existence when he met the three of them during the summer. And when he needed a room at the beginning of the semester, it didn't exactly seem like the best time to come clean with them.

What would he have told them anyway? *I really need a cheap place to live. And oh, by the way, remember everything I told you over the summer about being a poor kid from Boston? Well, it was all a sham. I'm really a rich kid from Boston.*

At the time it didn't seem like such a bad thing to fib a little about his family. He'd never actually said his family was poor. Just that he was poor. And that wasn't a lie. Sam had no money.

After another long, awkward silence Sam ventured to speak again. "Listen, Neil, I'm really sorry about misleading you guys. I never wanted it to turn out like this."

"Turn out like what?" Neil challenged him. "Like, for us to find out who you really are?"

"No, that's not it. I am who I am." Sam struggled to explain. "I never pretended to be someone I'm not. I mean, I'm still the same old Sam. I always have been. It's just that there are some things about my family that I don't feel all that comfortable with."

"Like the fact that they own the Sweet Valley Resort Hotel?" Neil asked pointedly.

"Well, yeah. And the fact that they're so rich."

"You mean, *you're* so rich," Neil corrected him. "You can't exactly separate yourself from your family's wealth, you know."

"I know," Sam agreed. "It isn't easy. But I've been trying. I haven't touched their money since I turned eighteen and split to be on my own. I am putting myself through OCC on scholarship. Why do you think I go to a school with such cheap tuition?"

"Right." Neil shot Sam a dubious look. "It must be hard having to survive on your trust fund, huh?"

"Listen, I don't even have a trust fund, okay?" Sam was getting frustrated, even though he had no right to be. And he was going to have to get used to answering questions like this. "I mean, one exists for me, yes, but I haven't gone near it, and I don't plan to."

"Hmmm." Neil didn't sound like he quite believed what Sam was telling him.

"It's true, Neil. I'm not just some rich kid who's slumming it, okay? I really am trying to make it on my own. And on my own terms."

Neil finally gave Sam his full attention for the first time since the conversation had begun. "Listen, Sam, you really don't owe me any explanations."

"But I do," Sam sputtered. "I owe everyone an explanation. I just don't want you guys all thinking I'm some kind of total fraud. Some parents disown their kids. I disowned my parents. That's all there is to it."

Sam took a deep breath. He wondered how that last bit was going to go down. Sam knew that Neil's parents had disowned him when he told them that he was gay. They'd cut him off from their lives and their money. What would Neil think of someone disowning their parents?

Neil regarded him. "Look, Sam, I'm sure you have your reasons for keeping your secrets. And that's good enough for me, buddy. Frankly, I don't care who your parents are or if they're poor or rich or what. But I think you know who you ought to be explaining yourself to."

"Elizabeth." Sam ran a nervous hand through his unruly sandy brown hair, imagining the difficulty he was going to face when he finally talked to Elizabeth.

"The one and only," Neil answered.

"I guess she's pretty upset, huh?" Sam could feel the dread in his voice.

"Yeah, I'd say *upset* is a pretty good way to describe how she's feeling."

Sam sighed. "Help me out, man. Should I talk to her tonight or wait till morning? What do you think?"

"That, my man, is up to you," Neil stated simply. He got up from his seat and headed for the kitchen, glancing over his shoulder at Sam, alone with the television. "Good luck."

Elizabeth turned on her side to check the digital alarm clock on her bedside table. The rectangular green numbers glowed 1:11. Time to make a wish, she thought glumly.

I wish I could get to sleep already, jeez. Better yet, I wish I never had met Sam Burgess in the first place.

Elizabeth was about to launch herself into an imaginary scenario where Sam Burgess didn't exist. But then she remembered: *You're supposed to make a wish at 11:11, not 1:11. Oh, well, my wishes never come true anyway.* The final digit blinked into a 2, and Elizabeth found herself reaching over to turn on her reading lamp.

170

Maybe if she read for a while, it would make her sleepy. It might even take her mind off Sam. He still hadn't come home, and now there was a part of her that hoped he never would. She picked up her copy of Thomas Wolfe's *You Can't Go Home Again* and smiled at the synchronicity between her thoughts and the objects around her. The smile disappeared at the sight of the fuzzy red journal that the Wolfe book had been sitting on.

She silently cursed Sam and cursed the stupid gift that had given rise to this whole mess she was in. The thoughtfulness of Sam's gesture had led her downstairs to thank him. The thank-you had led to the Kiss. And she had to think that it was the Kiss that sent Sam running to the safe haven of his parents' hotel. And to Anna.

If he had never given her the book, she never would have kissed him, and he never would have run away. Then she never would have gone searching for him and never would have found him half naked in a hotel room with his little squeeze, Anna. Sam's secret identity would have remained a secret, and Elizabeth would have been none the wiser. She would have been spared the humiliation of questioning the truth of every moment she had ever spent with Sam, of every feeling she had ever had for him. Every feeling she had ever sensed he had for her.

Again she found herself wishing Sam Burgess had

never been born. She eyed the journal as its fuzzy cover mocked her from the bedside table. All of a sudden the journal was an embodiment of Sam. Of Sam and all his lies. And she wanted to destroy it. Or at least get it as far away from her as possible. Which was exactly what she wished she could do to Sam.

Elizabeth picked up the journal and sat up in bed. In the soft yellow glow of her bedside lamp she held the book in both hands and stared at it with anger flashing in her eyes. And then she couldn't look at it for another second. She brought the book above her head with both hands and threw it as hard as she could. It hit her bedroom door with a thud and dropped to the floor.

A moment later she heard a light tapping on her door from the other side. Elizabeth quickly killed the light.

"Go away!" she shouted.

But before the words left her mouth, the door slowly opened, and there was Sam, backlit from the hallway light, a faint halo forming around his dark form.

"I said, go away!" Elizabeth blurted out, unsure of anything else to say.

But Sam wasn't going anywhere. "I'm sorry to barge in on you so late like this, Elizabeth, but I heard a noise—I guess it was this." Sam looked down and noticed the journal on the floor. He calmly picked it up and set it on top of the dresser by the window. "I know it's late, and I'm probably the last person you want to see right now, but we really need to talk."

Elizabeth's first instinct was to bury herself back beneath her big, warm comforter and scream at Sam again to go away, to leave her alone and never come back. But when she saw the utter confusion and desperation in his face, she knew she had to give him a chance. After all, this was the moment she'd been waiting for, wasn't it? Ever since she'd fled Sam's room after kissing him last week. And despite all that had happened since that night to make her feelings toward him change, Elizabeth knew she had to let Sam talk.

She collected her emotions as best she could and addressed him in a tone that conveyed her annoyance and distrust. "So, you're finally ready to talk now, huh, Sam? What did it take for you to come home? Me catching you at the Sweet Valley Resort Hotel with one of your little one-night stands? Or was it me finding out who you really are that brought you back here? That and what else? Another night of luxury at your parents' hotel, another day of relaxing by the pool with Anna, and, what, maybe five or six beers at Frankie's to give you the courage to face me?"

Sam's mouth opened, but no words came out.

He took a deep breath and tried again. "First of all, Elizabeth, I'm sorry I lied to you about who I am and where I'm from. I had no right to do that, and I realize that now. But I did have my reasons. And you've got to believe that I was never trying to deceive you."

"You never tried to deceive me?" Elizabeth repeated Sam's words in order to illustrate how ridiculous they sounded.

"Listen, Elizabeth, I—I'm serious," Sam stammered. "I have a lot of issues with my parents. And I guess in a lot of ways, I've been trying to pretend that they don't even exist. But before I go into any of that . . . before I go any further, I just want you to know that I haven't been sleeping with Anna."

"Oh, you haven't, have you?" Elizabeth was incredulous. "So the two of you were just enjoying a little breakfast in bed, but you didn't actually sleep together? And what about the time she stayed over at the duplex? I suppose you didn't sleep with her then either."

"Actually, no," Sam insisted implausibly. "I suppose that's another thing I have to level with you about."

Elizabeth was mildly curious to hear how Sam was going to cover up his relationship with Anna, but she wasn't about to sit there and let him continue to make a fool out of her. "Listen, Sam, I really don't have time for any more lies from you."

"I know, Elizabeth, I know," Sam responded adamantly. "And I'm not lying, I swear to you. In fact, all I want is to clear the air of all the lies I've told you in the past. Not that I'm some big liar; I'm really not. But I admit that I haven't been the most open and honest guy in the world. And if you'll just listen to me, maybe you'll be able to understand where I'm coming from."

"Okay, I'm listening." Elizabeth relented.

Sam paced back and forth in front of Elizabeth's bed as he spoke, and he had trouble looking her in the eye for more than a few seconds at a time.

"First of all, Anna and I are just friends," he began. "And that thing with her at the duplex. That was really all an act. You see, I had this idea when you were dating Finn—when I knew that he was messing around behind your back and when I knew you really liked him and that he was just trying to get you into bed—I had this idea that if I could somehow illustrate the way a guy like Finn treats women, then maybe you'd wake up to what he was all about."

Elizabeth was momentarily confused as she tried to connect her relationship with Finn to the night when Sam and Anna slept together at the house.

"So I convinced my friend Anna to help me

out," Sam continued, "by pretending to be some poor innocent girl I had lured into bed."

Sam must have sensed the horror Elizabeth felt as she began to understand what he was telling her because he stopped himself momentarily. "I know, it was a really stupid idea, and I probably shouldn't have done that either. But since you wouldn't believe me when I told you what Finn was up to, I thought that the only way to get through to you was by demonstrating the way guys like that really are."

Elizabeth could barely believe what Sam was telling her. "So you're saying that you and your little friend were just putting on an act to show *me* what my boyfriend was all about?"

"Um, yeah, basically," Sam admitted sheepishly.

Elizabeth was furious. "You know, Sam, you are really screwed up. Who do you think you are anyway? You have no right to go around putting on little acts and performances just so people will behave toward you the way you want them to. And there are no explanations that can justify all of your lies and betrayals. So why don't you just save your explanations and save your apologies and save your excuses and just stay out of my life!"

Sam stood staring at Elizabeth and shook his head. "Then I guess there's nothing I can say."

"I guess not." Elizabeth had plenty more to say herself, but she was afraid she'd start crying if she tried to talk. So she just sat with her lips pursed, shaking her own head slowly, and stared back at Sam. After a long, cold moment he silently turned and left the room, closing the door behind him and leaving Elizabeth alone in the dark once more.

A swift, warm breeze whirled around the gray-and-brown stone buildings of Sweet Valley University, setting the trees alive in a flurry of quivering branches and shaking leaves. Nina shivered and huddled herself together, not from a chill, but from doubt. Three hours at the mall and she had nothing to show for it but a headache and sore feet. Everything seemed wrong. She wasn't such an accomplished supershopper, she knew, but she hadn't been expecting the constant dissatisfaction she had faced with the many outfits she had inspected and tried on. And now she was beginning to realize that despite her initial enthusiasm over that evening's date with Josh, she really was completely uncertain over what was going on in her mind—and in her heart.

At first she had been excited and feeling flirty, and she had sorted through tight and revealing outfits. She had come close to buying a skimpy black tank top trimmed with beadwork and a short, bright red, gypsy-style skirt. Looking at herself in the mirror, she had done a little spin, feeling happy about the way the fabric's patterns played off her curves. Giggling to herself over how Josh would react to her natural but daring look, she had suddenly caught herself feeling exposed and unsafe. Sure, the sexy look would draw his attention and play up his desire, but was that what she wanted? What was the point of going out with him and heightening the desire and tension between them if all he was going to be thinking about was undressing her?

She didn't just want him to be pressuring her to go back up to his room from the beginning of their date. Oh, why hadn't she shown more restraint the other night and made him wait a little more patiently before having sex with him? He could have been wondering more about how she felt about him and making a greater effort to explore her feelings and ideas, and she in turn could have given him more of a chance to show himself. Now he would be expecting sex right from the start, and she knew that she would have a hard time believing that the things he said really showed his inner being. He might not even think he really had to try to please her, and she didn't want him to be lazy and complacent.

Doing a complete about-face in her shopping, Nina had tried on a pair of funky pink overalls over a burnt-orange, soft-cotton, long-sleeved tee. Her body was well hidden by the loose outfit, and the colors said fun but innocent. Nina had spent a long time staring in the three-way mirror in that outfit, and at first her imagination had reacted very positively to the way she looked: Without giving fuel to the fire of Josh's lust, she could picture his eyes focusing on hers and him actually listening closely to what she said and using his mind to draw out her ideas and dreams. Maybe it wasn't too late for them to make a deep connection before their relationship went any further. She had all but decided to go with it when a different sort of doubt stopped her.

She simply wasn't confident enough in Josh's feelings about her to count on his interest in her continuing to intensify without the appeal of a sexy and flirty attitude. She didn't think of it in those terms, of course—who did?—but again her imagination led the way. This time she imagined Josh as bored, as wanting to get back to his room shortly after the movie but alone, to study. She knew that he wasn't caught up with his work, and she could all too easily imagine him writing off the evening as a washout and deciding to devote his energy to more mundane and less personal matters.

From that point on, every outfit she had tried

on had left her full of doubt one way or the other. If it wasn't sexy enough, she pictured him losing interest. If it was exciting, she pictured him having too much interest, the wrong kind of interest. Eventually she had realized the futility of her mission, and she had left the mall empty-handed, returning to SVU in defeat.

The problem, she realized, wasn't clothes. It was Josh. Nina felt more completely than ever at a loss over what to think about him, about what he thought about her. She just had no way to read him, to discern from what he had said and done what he might be thinking about her, where he was hoping things between them would go. She knew what she thought about him: He was a good guy, probably the right kind of guy for her, with his easygoing lifestyle and serious attitude toward school.

It was easy to imagine the two of them being together for a long time, learning together, supporting each other through the demands of their studies. But she also knew that guys were often not inclined to think in the long term and that they might do or say anything if they thought it meant they might "score." Nina shivered with displeasure at the idea. Why did girls always have to watch out for this gross possibility when contemplating the motives of that strange species, the young adult human male?

And of course, you couldn't just *ask*. In science any question was appropriate: If you wanted to know something, you could just look in a book, or do an experiment, or sometimes just think about it. But no amount of thought was going to clear up these doubts in her mind, and gathering data involved the very sorts of experiments that she was trying to avoid.

But the worst of it was that she was sure that somewhere, in his heart of hearts, Josh knew perfectly well what he was thinking about her. Conquest or soul mate? If it was the former, he'd never admit it, of course, and if he *was* thinking about her in a long-term way, he would be afraid to talk about it. It was just the nature of the beast: Boys were always making sure they kept girls at some distance to protect their much valued independence.

Something kept them from pursuing meaningful relationships even if they really wanted one. Everyone knew that. It was a paradox, but there was nothing to be done to solve it. You just had to wait and see and try to keep from getting hurt. And that was so hard, Nina thought. Maybe she wasn't up for it. Maybe she should just cancel their date and avoid him. But then she'd just be back where she started, alone, and that was no good either. Nothing worked.

Nina's head was beginning to spin. She felt that she had never been so confused over anything in all her life. And confusion wasn't something she was used to, not something she was good at. She stopped in her tracks, looking up into the wind-blown trees, where songbirds were struggling against the breeze to keep their perches or trying to navigate the tricky currents as they flitted about. *They live by instinct,* she thought. She was jealous.

Just then out of the corner of her eye Nina saw a familiar figure. She turned for a closer look: It was Dan, a guy who lived on Josh's floor. Josh had called him a friend. He had seemed nice too when they had met and more polite than the typical beer-swilling macho dorks who seemed to inhabit most of the dorms. Sensitive, almost. Human anyway. He saw her too and with a little wave began to walk her way. Nina smiled and waved back and walked toward him to meet him halfway.

"Hi, Dan," she said lightly.

"Nina. How's it going? Any major discoveries today?"

"No, not yet, but the day is young. Maybe in lab this afternoon." Nina liked being thought of as a brain sometimes.

"Well, goodness knows we could use one. So what's new? Going to that Hitchcock thing tonight?"

"Yeah, Josh and I are going after dinner. I hope it's not too scary."

"Yeah. I wish I could go, but I'm rewriting a paper. My philosophy prof is such a stickler! I just spent two hours in the library, trying to read his comments on my rough draft. He makes me feel like I don't understand anything."

"Ouch."

"Yeah, ouch. But at least he reads the papers. It's more than I can say for my English prof. Anyway, I'm going to try to recover a little before sitting down to write. But I see a long night ahead of me at the computer."

Nina saw a chance to gather a little data. Maybe she could feel Dan out to see if Josh had said anything about her to him—and if he had revealed his own feelings about her. It was kind of a long shot, she thought, considering how bad most guys were about talking about their feelings, but it was worth a try. And besides, she could use something hot and sweet. "How about a coffee on me, Dan? A little brain juice might get you thinking in the right direction."

"Hey, that's a great idea," Dan said with a smile. "Thanks. Yum-Yum's?"

"Sure."

Chapter
Twelve

It was a beautiful day. Ordinarily Jessica would have been happy to be walking through campus on an afternoon like this. The sun was shining, birds were chirping, and even the squirrels looked cute, chasing one another through the branches high above the walkways of SVU. And speaking of cute, the hotties were out in force. Jessica might have been content to find a quiet spot on the lawn and simply watch the guys walk by, smiling at the especially fine ones, and wait for one of them to join her for a chat in the grass. But right now she just had too much on her mind.

That kiss she shared with Jason yesterday was intense. Then again, when Neil appeared in the doorway, things got even more intense—and not in a good way. Every time her mind drifted so sweetly to Jason's soft, gentle lips pressed against her mouth, the image abruptly dissolved into Neil standing in the doorway, a look of horror dangling from his face.

Why did things have to be so difficult with guys all of a sudden? Part of her wished that she had been wrong about Jason from the start. Part of her wished that he *was* gay. But after yesterday whatever minuscule doubts that had floated in the back of her mind were utterly washed away.

She'd been elated to discover that Jason liked her, was attracted to her. But at what expense? At the expense of her best friend.

But I didn't steal him away from anyone! Jessica insisted to herself again. *Neil never had a chance with him in the first place. And if he would have listened to me, he never would have put himself in the position to have his heart broken like that.*

But the facts remained. And they were written all over the crestfallen face of Neil that kept surfacing in Jessica's mind every time she imagined Jason's shining eyes and warm, supple lips. If only she could see Jason again, not in her thoughts, but in the flesh, she might be able to forget the heartache she had caused Neil.

Or maybe she wouldn't be able to, and then at least she'd know that there could be no future between her and Jason. Because no matter how great Jason was, if being with him was going to always remind her of the hurt she had caused her best friend, then no kisses in the world would be enough to make her feel good about herself.

Jessica glanced across one of the lawns at a rush of students pouring forth from the science building. As if she had conjured him with her mind, she spotted Jason among them. Dressed in charcoal stretch-denim jeans and a tight black T-shirt, he was a vision of simplicity and beauty, oblivious to Jessica's gaze from afar. At first sight her heart went *ping*, and she was tempted to go to him.

She could wind around the walkway and pretend to be running into him when their paths crossed. But then the image of Neil's broken face flashed into her mind, and she knew there was no use pursuing Jason. Sure, he was beautiful. And strong and smart and sensitive, and he seemed like he had his life together. If her friend Neil weren't an issue, then Jason would be the perfect guy for Jessica right now. But Neil most certainly was an issue, and she couldn't get beyond that. He was more than an issue; he was her best friend. And no guy—not even one as great as Jason—was going to come between them.

With that conclusion made, there was no way Jessica could go after Jason right now. She had to find Neil and smooth things out between them. As she turned around to head back home, Jessica spotted Chloe and Martin coming toward her. She couldn't help thinking how cute they looked together: status-obsessed Chloe in her trendy clothes and down-to-earth Martin in brown corduroys and a dorky jacket.

"Hi, Jessica," Chloe sang out. "How's it going?"

"Hey, Chloe," Jessica greeted her. She smiled at Martin as they came to a stop in front of her.

Even though they were less than two feet away, Martin raised his hand in an awkward wave. "Hi, Jessica, remember me? I'm Martin, Chloe's boyfriend."

Chloe blushed and jabbed Martin lightly with her elbow. "Martin, we're just *friends!*" She looked at Jessica and rolled her eyes. "You're forgetting the whole conversation we had last night!"

"Hi, Martin," Jessica offered cheerfully, trying to make up for Chloe's dissing him in front of her. "Of course I remember you. We met at Yum-Yum's."

"Exactly," Martin confirmed, smiling happily at Jessica and seeming completely unfazed by Chloe's rude comment.

Chloe shuffled her feet, evidently embarrassed by Martin. *What a shame*, Jessica thought. *What a stupid shame*. Here was this perfectly nice guy who liked Chloe, who wanted to be her boyfriend, and here Chloe was, wanting something else that was just an idea: a cool boyfriend.

You're immature, Chloe, Jessica wanted to scream. *You're as immature as I used to be. But stuff'll happen that'll make you grow up. You'll see.*

Jessica's mind wandered back to her own complicated love life. If only she could be in denial like Chloe. But what was the point in that? If you wanted to be with someone, you wanted to be with them no matter what anyone else thought. Including your sorority sisters and including your best friend. And that was why Jessica knew she could never be with Jason. Because no matter how badly she wanted him, she would always care too much about how their relationship would make Neil feel.

And that was why she needed to go find Neil now. To let him know that there would be no relationship between her and Jason.

"Jessica, is everything all right?" Chloe asked in a tone of concern. "You seem so distracted."

"Yeah, I guess I am," Jessica admitted. "But I feel fine, really. It's just that I sort of have some things I need to take care of right now. No offense, but I should probably get going."

"Sure, no problem," Chloe answered understandingly.

"Is there anything we can do for you?" Martin offered innocently.

189

Chloe hit him with another light jab of her elbow. "Martin."

"No, that's okay, but thanks," Jessica replied sincerely. "This is something I need to take care of on my own."

"Well, good luck," Martin offered hopefully.

"Thanks, Martin." Jessica reached forward and touched his arm. "I'll see you guys around, all right? Bye, Chloe."

"Bye, Jessica." Chloe smiled and added pleasantly, "I hope everything works out."

Jessica walked away and could hear Chloe scolding Martin about his manners. Poor deluded girl! She'd found a gem, and she didn't know it!

Now if only Jessica could find someone perfect for *her*. Someone who wouldn't cause problems between her and Neil. But for now anyway she'd be happy if she could just keep Neil as a friend.

Nina sipped her hot chocolate slowly so as not to burn her tongue and watched Dan as he emptied four packets of sugar into his latte. He looked up, a little embarrassed. "It's good this way," he murmured.

"So, Dan, how long have you and Josh been friends?" Nina wanted to get straight to the point.

"Friends? I just met him this year in the dorm. He's a good guy. We play computer games together." He winced a little after saying that. "Sorry, that's geeky, isn't it?"

"I don't think so," Nina said honestly. "They're hard. Most people don't have the patience."

"Yeah, it's true. But some of us don't really have the time either."

"Do you think Josh is as patient as you are?"

"Josh?" he repeated, as if he'd never heard the name before. "Uh, I don't know. He's pretty smart, though. He gets the idea quicker than I do usually."

"Do you guys play the same game for a long time?"

"Well, sometimes, I guess. But when I start to catch up, he wants to change games. You know, to keep winning. He likes to keep me on my toes."

"Hmmm. Maybe you should figure out the game before you start playing with him."

"Nah," he said modestly. "That's no fun. It's okay. I don't care that much if he wins. I just like to play."

Nina took another sip of her hot chocolate. Dan was seeming more and more like a nice guy. She thought she could probably trust him with a more direct question. "Do you know if Josh has had a lot of girlfriends?"

"A lot?" he repeated again. "Yeah, I don't know, I'd say a lot. More than me anyway. Compared to me, he's Leonardo DiCaprio."

Nina laughed. "Don't say that, Dan. There's only one Leo."

"Okay, then, I don't know. Ben Affleck."

Nina steered the conversation back to her intended inquiry. "Do you guys talk about girls?"

"Girls? Yeah, no, I don't know. Sometimes. We talk about you sometimes."

Nina carefully tried not to show her interest. She hid her pursed lips behind the oversized cup of cocoa. "What's he say anyway?"

"He really likes you, Nina. He says you're, like, the coolest chick—I'm sorry, the coolest woman—he's met in a long time."

Nina felt a warm flush growing from her stomach out to her fingers and toes. "Oh, yeah? Tell me more."

"Well, he says you're really smart, you know, like really good in science and stuff. And for a long time he couldn't stop talking about how pretty he thinks you are." Dan's ears turned red, and he paused to stir his coffee more carefully. "Yeah, I probably liked you a whole lot before you and I even met. I was pretty jealous of Josh. He always seems to meet cool girls—I mean, women."

"Well," Nina said happily, "I wouldn't worry about it if I were you, Dan. You seem like a pretty cool guy yourself." It felt good to give him a little ego boost. Poor guy probably needed it.

"Do you think so?" Dan asked eagerly. "Wow."

"I think a lot of girls would be happy to go out with you."

"Wow." Dan inspected his spoon carefully. His ears were bright red, and he fidgeted in his seat. He looked like he was wrestling with some difficult internal question. "We should hang out sometime maybe," he finally managed to utter.

"Sure," Nina said. "Maybe next time you and Josh are playing computer games, I could join in."

Dan looked more uncomfortable than ever. "I mean, like, go out to a movie or dinner or something. You know, in the evening."

Nina was puzzled. Where was this coming from? "You mean, like a date?"

"Well." Dan sounded like he had been caught doing something illicit. "Yeah. You know, if you want to, we could go out sometime."

Nina's puzzlement turned to shock. What kind of a friend was this, trying to steal a girlfriend? Maybe he was even more clueless than he made himself out to be. "Dan," she said gently, "you seem nice, really, but don't you think Josh might not like that?"

"Oh, no," Dan offered eagerly. "Don't worry. I asked him."

"You what?"

"I was complaining about not being able to meet girls—I mean, uh, women—and that I wished I could ask you out. He said it was okay. You know, since you guys are just casual, that if I liked you so much, I should go for it."

Nina's heart practically stopped. She couldn't believe what she was hearing. "Casual?"

"Yeah, you know, that you have an understanding that it's not going to be serious. Like, you're seeing other people and stuff."

Nina was now completely flustered. She felt like her stomach had turned to lead. *Oh, no*, she thought. *This is horrible. No. Too horrible for horrible*. "Other . . . people?" she croaked.

"Yeah, you know! Like, if you meet someone else, no big deal. No strings." Dan smiled cluelessly, apparently thinking that this question was going better than he had expected. "So, you know, since we get along, how about me? You met me. I'm someone else. Whaddaya say?" He beamed at her tight face, her quivering lip, her moistening eyes. "Nina?" He stopped himself. "Are you okay? It's all right if you want to say no."

Nina was almost unable to speak. "N-N-No, it's . . . it's . . ." She trailed off. She had to get out of there. She stood up and fished in her purse for her wallet. Her fingers weren't working, and she couldn't see through the tears that were now starting to overflow.

Dan finally got a clue. He stood up awkwardly, twisting his hands. "Aw, jeez, Nina, I'm sorry. I must have got that wrong. Look, forget it. I said the wrong thing. Don't let's tell Josh, okay? You guys are good together. We should hang out, you know, uh . . ." He was at a loss. "Play computer games," he offered lamely.

Nina found a five-dollar bill and dropped it on the table. Tears were rolling off her chin and dropping on the table like raindrops. She tried to tell Dan it wasn't his fault and to let the waitress keep the change, but it was no good. Her mind was almost a complete blank. Without another word she ran out of the café blindly, almost knocking over another table.

Jessica walked in the front door of the duplex and called Neil's name. She was finally ready to put the whole Jason situation to rest.

"I'm up here, Jess," he called from his room.

Jessica mounted the stairs and walked straight into Neil's room, hoping in her heart that he would forgive her for what he had witnessed the day before.

"Neil, I have some things I need to tell you," she began. "But first I guess I owe you an explanation for what happened in Jason's room yesterday."

Neil turned in his desk chair to face Jessica, but he didn't exactly look happy to see her. "Yeah, well, it looked pretty self-explanatory to me."

"I know it looked bad, but please, just listen to me," Jessica pleaded. "The whole reason I went to see Jason yesterday was to tell him it was over between us—not that it had ever really started in the first place. But I knew how much he means to you, and I had finally decided to stop getting in the way of you going after him."

"So what happened?" Neil asked dubiously.

"Well, to tell you the truth, once I got there, I felt pretty silly. I mean, I wasn't going to tell him it had anything to do with you, but I was really ready to break things off." Jessica spoke quickly, her thoughts immediately forming themselves into words. "But then I started thinking about it, and I was like, how do you break up with someone when you've never even kissed them before?"

"Oh, I get it. So you were going to kiss him and then break up with him."

Jessica knew Neil wasn't serious, but she could tell he wasn't joking around either. "No, of course that isn't it. But once I got there, I guess I kind of lost my nerve to say what I was going to say. And besides, he looked soooo good, and then, I don't know, I had made up my mind that even if I didn't say it in so many words, I just wasn't going to call him, or see him, or talk to him ever again—at least until you and he were able to work things out. But then we started talking, and all of sudden he was getting closer and closer, and before I knew it, he was kissing me."

Neil looked doubtful. "He was kissing you, or you were kissing him?"

"*He* kissed *me*, I swear, Neil," Jessica insisted. "That's how it started. But then it felt so good that I just couldn't stop. And then you showed up."

"Right." Neil frowned. "I showed up and ruined the whole thing."

"No, you didn't. In fact, I think you showed up for a reason," Jessica tried to explain.

"Yes, I showed up for a reason," Neil repeated impatiently. "Jason and I had plans to hang out. That's the reason."

"No, I think it was more than just that. I think you needed to see what you saw. And I'm not saying I planned this in any way because I didn't." Jessica took a breath and continued. "But I just don't think you would have ever believed the truth about Jason unless you saw it with your own eyes."

Neil's face filled with anger. "Is this what you came in here to tell me, Jessica? *See, I told you so?*"

"No, Neil, no. That's not it at all," Jessica persisted. "The truth is, I've been doing a lot of thinking. And I had already decided this before anything happened yesterday. And despite what *did* happen, I still feel the same way. I don't want to come between you and Jason—whether he's straight or gay; I don't care. And even more important, I don't want Jason to come between us. I love you, Neil. You're the best friend I've got. And I don't want to lose you."

Neil's angry expression gave way to a soft smile.

He got up from his chair and walked toward her.

"Jessica, you're probably not going to believe this," he began, looking her in the eye, "but I've come to the same conclusion myself. Whether Jason is gay or straight; it doesn't matter to me anymore. All that matters is that you and I remain friends. And if you really like him, then go for it. I'm not going to stand in your way any longer."

Jessica could tell that Neil was telling the truth. And it was exactly what she wanted to hear. But somehow, even with Neil's blessing to go after Jason, she found herself feeling no longer interested. All that mattered now was getting her friendship with Neil back on track.

"You know what? You can have him." Jessica smiled wider than she had in weeks and stepped forward to give Neil a hug. As they embraced, Jessica was finally happy to be with the guy who mattered most in her life: her best friend.

"So, now that we're friends again, why don't we celebrate?" Neil proposed, still holding tight to Jessica.

"Dancing at Starlights tonight?" Jessica suggested.

"You read my mind," Neil answered.

Jessica let go of Neil and gave him a goofy grin. "That's what friends are for."

Then she kissed him on the cheek, and they hugged again.

Chapter
Thirteen

Sam pulled into the parking lot of Anna's building. He glanced down at the two beautiful bouquets— one of yellow lilies and purple irises and the other of simple white daisies—beside him on the passenger's seat.

Finally he was ready to make things right, first with Anna and then with Elizabeth. And what better way to grease the wheels of forgiveness than fresh flowers? Sam still didn't think that Anna was ready to face him after her blowup on Monday morning and especially since he hadn't quite managed to tell Elizabeth how he felt, and he wasn't sure if he was ready to speak to her either. Anna, that was. Elizabeth, he knew he had to face.

So in case he didn't have the nerve to knock on Anna's door, he brought a short note he had written that morning:

Dear Anna,

Here's a small token of my appreciation for all you've done for me. Thanks so much for listening the other night. And thanks for the advice. I'm finally ready to do the right thing with Elizabeth. I'll let you know how things turn out. If that makes me the kind of guy you want to know again.

Love,

Sam

Sam raised his hand to knock on Anna's door but couldn't quite gather the strength. He was afraid that explaining himself to one girl was all he could manage today. So he knelt down and gently placed the bunch of daisies on her doorstep along with the note. He turned and walked away, shifting his thoughts to what he could possibly say to Elizabeth.

He had hardly gone four steps when he heard the door whoosh open behind him.

"Ahem, I think you're forgetting something, mister." It was Anna, and she was bending down to pick up the flowers, plucking up the small white envelope along with them.

Sam was embarrassed. Like he was caught in the act of doing something wrong, not making a sweet gesture to someone he cared about. "Oh, um, those are for you, Anna."

"Why, they're beautiful." Anna stuck her nose in the bouquet and inhaled deeply. "But I don't think I heard you knock."

"Well, uh, I guess that's because I didn't," Sam admitted.

"And why not?"

"I wasn't sure if you'd really want to see me. So I just thought I'd leave those for you with a little note. You can read it if you want."

"Why don't you just tell me what it says, and then I won't have to?"

"I just wanted to thank you for being there for me the other night, that's all." Sam paused. "And to let you know that I'm going to finally follow your advice."

"Now, that wasn't so hard, was it, Sam?"

"What do you mean?" Sam asked innocently.

"What I mean is, talking to someone face-to-face," Anna elaborated, "instead of leaving little notes and flowers and then running away."

"Well, I wasn't exactly *running*," Sam replied defensively.

"You know what I mean, Sam," Anna said, pointing the daisies at him accusingly. "And something tells me that you have another bouquet and little note out in your car for a certain Ms.

Wakefield . . . unless you've already left it on her doorstep."

Sam swallowed. How did Anna know him so well? "Okay, I do have a bouquet for her."

"Sam, you have to go and talk to her," Anna ordered him. "I mean, you can bring her flowers if you want, but that's never going to take the place of the truth."

"I am going to talk to her," Sam promised. "I even tried to talk to her last night. But I was barely able to even explain that night you and I spent together at the duplex before she ordered me out of her room. And, I'm afraid, out of her life."

"You can't let that stop you," Anna urged him. "You still have to tell Elizabeth the truth, whether she says she wants to hear it or not. You owe her that. And you owe it to yourself too."

"I know, I know. You're right. And I am planning to talk to her. In fact, I spent all last night and most of today just thinking about everything she said to me. And what I'm going to say to her."

"What *are* you going to say to her?" Anna pressed.

"Well, first I'm going to apologize to her— again—for all the lies and deceit I've put her through." Sam stopped to think some more about what he had to say. "And, um, I guess I'm going to finally admit to her that there's something

202

between us—between me and Elizabeth, I mean—that's still real, no matter how many lies I've told about myself. And that we both owe it to each other, and to ourselves, to acknowledge our true feelings. And that hopefully, we can start all over again."

"That sounds like a good start," Anna said encouragingly. "Now, what are you waiting for? Get going."

With his resolve finally steeled, Sam got in his car and drove straight home to confront Elizabeth. He was glad that Anna had caught him before he left and that they'd had their little chat. Somehow talking to Anna about what he wanted to say bolstered his courage.

He pulled up in front of the house and grabbed the bouquet off the seat. Sam ran up the steps and burst through the front door, afraid he might lose his nerve if he hesitated at all. Once inside the house, he raced up the stairs to Elizabeth's room. The door was open! Thank goodness he wouldn't have to knock and be told to go away again.

But when he peered inside, no one was there.

Nina slid the coins into the pay phone and crossed her fingers. *Please be home,* she prayed as she dialed Elizabeth's number.

The phone began to ring.

Please be home, Nina prayed again as the tears slipped down her cheeks. As a bus drove by, Nina plugged her ear with her finger.

"Hello?"

"Neil?" Nina asked.

"Yup," he replied. "Who's this? Oh, Nina, right?"

"Right," she barely managed.

"Hang on a sec, okay?" Neil told her. "I'll see if Liz's upstairs."

"Eliz-a-beth!" he screamed at the top of his lungs.

Nina held the receiver away from her ear.

"Hello?"

Nina was never so happy to hear another person's voice. She heard Neil hang up his extension. "Elizabeth, it's me, Nina." That was as far as she could get before she burst into tears.

"Nina? Honey?" Elizabeth said. "What's the matter?"

"I . . . it . . . ," Nina spluttered, the tears coming faster than her speech.

"Sweetheart, where are you?" Elizabeth asked. "Just tell me where you are, and I'll come meet you."

"I'm around the corner from Yum-Yum's, at a pay phone," Nina said.

"Okay. Nina, are you listening?"

Nina nodded. "Yes," she thought to croak into the phone.

"Go to Yum-Yum's, toward the back where it tends to be quiet. I'll meet you there in ten minutes, okay?"

"Okay," Nina said, and hung up. She pulled a tissue out of her knapsack and blew her nose. Then she pulled out her compact and checked her face.

You look like a wreck, she told herself, wiping at her dripping mascara. *Everything is going to be okay. Elizabeth's coming to meet you. So pull yourself together, go back into Yum-Yum's with your head bowed, and sneak into the back of the café.*

Everything's gonna be fine, she told herself again as she started walking back toward Yum-Yum's.

But then she saw Dan skulking around the corner, away from her and toward his dorm.

And she burst into tears again.

Neil looked himself over approvingly in the bathroom mirror as he worked a small glob of gel into his dark hair. Suddenly Jessica's reflection appeared beside his own. And for the first time in at least a week, he didn't feel like smacking her when he saw her. With her golden blond hair resting on her shoulders, her lips glowing a brilliant red, and, for once, a warm rather than mischievous smile emblazoned on her face, she looked gorgeous.

"So, I see you're using my hair gel without asking," Jessica teased.

"I tell you, this stuff is the best," Neil declared as he snapped the spout closed on top of the large, white plastic container. "Nothing holds like it."

"Yeah, and you can buy the next tube since you're using mine all up." Jessica grabbed it from him. "So, do you want to get a bite to eat before we go dancing?" she inquired.

"Sure," Neil agreed. "What did you have in mind?"

"Well, if you don't feel like cooking for us," Jessica began slyly, "I heard about this new Japanese noodle place. It's supposed to be good, and it's not that far from Starlights."

"Japanese noodles, huh?" Neil was less than enthusiastic.

"Yeah, come on, Neil. You've got to try new things. I've heard it's really good. Plus it's cheap."

"If it's good and cheap, then why not? As long as you don't make me eat any raw fish."

"All right, no sushi," Jessica promised. "So we should probably get going soon, right?"

"Yeah, okay," Neil said, suddenly distracted by the ringing telephone.

His stomach jumped as he wondered if it might be Jason calling. Even though he had worked things out with Jessica over the whole Jason situation, he hadn't talked to Jason himself. They had exchanged curt hellos at the econ exam, but it didn't exactly seem like the time to hash things out. And Jason had finished before him and left the room without saying anything. Neil had been half hoping—and half dreading—that Jason would be waiting outside for him, but when he left the building, there was no sign of him.

The phone rang again, and Neil practically raced to his room to answer it. Thankfully, Jessica didn't try to get it herself.

"Hello?" Neil could feel the nervous tremor in his voice.

"Hey, Neil, it's me, Jason," he announced cheerfully.

"Oh, hi, Jason." Neil tried to modulate his voice so that he sounded neither anxious nor angry.

"Neil, about what happened yesterday . . . ," he began awkwardly.

Neil cut him off nervously. "Really, you don't need to say anything."

Jason sounded just as anxious on the other end of the line. "Actually, I think I do. Listen, this isn't easy for me, but I think I need to explain some things—to you as well as Jessica."

"Me *and* Jessica?" Neil clarified, noticing Jessica in his doorway, tilting her head curiously. "Are you sure?"

"Yeah, listen." Jason's voice wavered as he continued. "I feel like I haven't been very straightforward with either of you, and, well, what happened yesterday in my room was a big mistake."

"It was?" Neil couldn't hide his surprise and was suddenly self-conscious as he looked at Jessica, listening to only half of the conversation. He wondered if he had been right about Jason after all.

"Yes, it was a big mistake," Jason repeated. "But I really think I owe it to both of you to explain this to you in person. Is Jessica around?"

"Uh, yeah," Neil answered hesitantly. "Do you want to talk to her?"

Jessica started reaching for the phone, but Neil put up his hand until Jason answered his question.

"No, not right now. But I would like to meet up with you, with both of you. Are you guys busy right now?"

Neil waved Jessica away from the phone. "Well, we *were* just about to go out, but if you really want to get together, maybe we could meet somewhere?"

Neil looked at Jessica as her eyes widened in a combination of surprise and curiosity.

"Yeah, that sounds good. How about Yum-Yum's?

We can have some tea or something, then I can tell you guys together what I need to say. How long do you need to get there?"

"I don't know, a half hour?" Neil proposed, looking toward Jessica for approval. She nodded, although she was obviously still confused about what was happening.

"Sounds perfect. I'll see you both there in half an hour." He was about to hang up but then added, as if an afterthought, "Neil, I'm really sorry about what happened yesterday—you know, not getting together to study and everything. Things have just been a little crazy for me lately. But I'll explain everything when I see you, okay?"

"Okay, I guess we'll see you soon, then. Bye." Neil hung up the phone and looked at Jessica with his lower lip curled down in perplexity.

Jessica looked equally nonplussed. "So what was that all about?"

Neil shrugged. "He says he wants to talk to both of us and that he has a lot to explain."

Neil decided to leave out the part about what happened yesterday being a big mistake. Now that he and Jessica had smoothed things out, he didn't want to return to their previous state of catdom.

"What does he want to talk about?" Jessica demanded. "What else did he say?"

"That's about it," Neil offered. "He just said that he hasn't been straightforward with either one of us and that he wants to explain everything in person."

"Well." Jessica shrugged. "I guess we'll find out soon enough."

"Yeah, I guess so." Neil put his arm around Jessica, and they walked downstairs together.

Elizabeth stepped tentatively into the semigloom of Yum-Yum's Café, her eyes skimming over the sea of unfamiliar faces. Finally, in the back of the room, Nina appeared. Her usually cheerful face was downcast, her eyes staring unseeingly at the cup in front of her. She stirred her coffee listlessly. Elizabeth was troubled by her appearance but also very glad to see her friend. *There she is,* Elizabeth thought. *Oh, Nina, what have they done to you?*

Putting on her best smile, she stepped carefully among the tables. Nina's eyes perked up when she saw her and then grew anxious again. She looked unsure of anything. Elizabeth walked past the empty chair and put her hand on Nina's shoulder. "Hi," she said softly, and crouched beside her. Nina looked into her eyes, and Elizabeth could see that she'd been crying.

"Oh, Elizabeth," she said. "I'm so sorry."

"Nina," Elizabeth said calmly. "You have nothing to be sorry about. It was my fault."

"No," Nina protested. "I was a complete jerk to you. I don't know what's wrong with me these days." She looked fearful and tired.

Elizabeth put her arms around Nina's shoulders and hugged her, holding Nina's cheek to hers. "Stop it with that," she said. "C'mon." She could feel Nina's body relax, and she stayed still, in her crouch, holding her friend close to her. "Everything's going to be all right."

"Thanks," Nina whispered. "I'm so glad you're here."

"Me too," Elizabeth said gently. She clasped Nina's hands between hers and looked into her eyes again. Nina looked comforted but still vulnerable. "How's the coffee today?" Elizabeth asked.

"I don't know," Nina said. "I don't know anything."

Elizabeth sat down opposite her and leaned over the table. "What's going on?" she asked.

Nina told her about her conversation with Dan, delaying before she got to the part where Dan had told her what Josh had said about their relationship. Elizabeth looked at her friend with disbelief. "He told him that he could ask you out? Are you kidding?"

"I wish I was. But he's too simple to have made it up. He couldn't even tell how horrible it was, what he was saying." Nina smiled ironically. "It was obviously true. Josh doesn't care about me at all. He was trying to pass me around! Can you believe that?"

Elizabeth frowned grimly. "I wish I could say no. But it happens sometimes. Some guys just have no clue at all. This Josh sounds like a grade-A specimen."

"Yeah, well, I had no clue either. I thought that there was really something there, you know? It seemed like we were getting along great, like we could make it work out. I mean, we had so much in common, and we got along so well, and he could be so nice sometimes. But I was so, so wrong. Oh, Elizabeth, I hurt so bad."

Elizabeth was filled with compassion for Nina. Her recent travails with the mystery of Sam Burgess seemed trivial in comparison. She could handle a jerky guy—she'd known a lot of them. But poor Nina! She was just learning the rules of the game.

Elizabeth thought back to her days at Sweet Valley High, finding out that guys could seem to feel one way while really they were just trying to use her. Between her friends and her constant comparisons with Jessica's experiences, it hadn't been that bad. She had usually been a step ahead. She'd had her share of heartbreak, of course—the devious Finn Robinson being a perfect case in point—but she knew that Nina was getting hit very hard by this fiasco. She wished she could say something that would help, but she was pretty sure that there was nothing to be done but to let the healing hand of time do its work. "Well," she offered, "at least you got out of it before you got too involved."

"Yeah." Nina didn't sound convinced. "I just wish . . . I just wish . . ." She fell silent, twisting a paper napkin between her fingers.

"You wish he'd been straight with you? Oh, honey, you never get that."

"No, Elizabeth, I wish I hadn't slept with him!" Tears started to well in her eyes.

Elizabeth was startled. She hadn't known Nina had slept with Josh! The poor girl. Elizabeth felt a pang of guilt in her stomach like a knife. While she had been playing girl detective in the long soap opera with Sam, Nina was laying it all out on the line—and losing big. "Nina," she said firmly but gently, taking Nina's twisting hand in hers, "forget about it. Okay? Sex isn't everything. Sometimes it doesn't happen at the right time or in the right way, but when it goes wrong, you can't obsess over it. It happened. You were careful, weren't you?"

Nina nodded.

"Then try to put it out of your mind."

"I can't," Nina whispered. "I feel so used. Dirty. Stupid. I'm so stupid!" She slapped her forehead. The tears were trailing slowly down her cheeks.

Elizabeth took the offending hand in hers and held her friend's hands together on the table with her hand. With the other she dabbed at Nina's tears with a napkin. "No, you're not, Nina. Don't say that. You're human. You're a good person. You're the smartest person I know. So you slept with him! That doesn't make you a fool. That means you were willing to try, to believe. It's not so easy to tell who the good ones are, huh?"

Nina laughed through her tears, choking a little. She looked relieved. Not as relieved as Elizabeth, though. She was so happy to see Nina laugh that all her concern about Sam and her guilt over ignoring Nina faded into unimportance. She wanted Nina to be happy so much. She vowed silently never to desert her again. She was always going to be there for her friend, she swore to herself.

Elizabeth squeezed Nina's hands. "Welcome to the club, sister," she intoned. "You've passed the initiation. Trial by fire. You picked a tough one, but it's behind you now, okay?" Nina was impassive. "Okay?" Elizabeth repeated, looking pleadingly at her.

Nina nodded slightly and shifted in her seat. She took her hands away from Elizabeth and reached for a sip of her coffee. She seemed more under control. Elizabeth felt a deep happiness, born out of her closeness and love for her friend. She felt as close to her in that moment as she had ever felt toward her own sister.

"So," Nina said softly. "What's this big story about Sam anyway?"

"Oh, that." Elizabeth smiled. It seemed so small to her now. "Well, our little rebel isn't quite what he appears to be. Not at all. Working-class tough? Hardly. Nina, he's rich. Not a little rich either, but, like, really, really rich. His parents own the Sweet Valley Resort Hotel. And a dozen other hotels, I think. And who knows what else. Maybe they're, like, from some old Boston aristocratic family, if they're even from Boston. But definitely not poor or even middle-class, that's for sure."

"Oh my God," Nina whispered. "I can't believe it."

"I wouldn't have believed it myself if I hadn't seen it with my own eyes. He didn't come home for days, and I got worried about him, so I was driving all over town. And then I see his car in the parking lot of the hotel, so I go in to see if he's staying there for some reason. And he is. In the owner's suite. Because he's the owner. Can you believe that? So I go to confront him and see what's going on or whatever, and guess what? He's not there alone. He's got some girl with him—Anna, this girl he was fooling around with a couple of weeks ago."

Nina looked concerned. "So what did you do?"

"I got out of there is what I did! Who needs to stick around for a phony like that? I mean, I'm sorry, but Sam is a bigger jerk than I ever would have thought."

"Why, just because he hid his past? I can kind of understand that. Why are you so upset?"

215

"Just wait. That's not the worst of it. He comes to see me last night and tells me this big story about how he and Anna are 'just friends'—even though they're, like, sleeping in the same room at the hotel, and were sleeping in his room at the duplex before, and I like totally saw them making out. And why? Nina, he said they were faking it—for me. For me. So I wouldn't be hung up on Finn. So I could see that some guys are just interested in sex. Like he was going to scare me out of it by acting like a jerk around Anna, as if that was supposed to mean anything to me."

Nina was gaping at Elizabeth. "That's unbelievable."

Elizabeth smiled with satisfaction. "I know, right? What a crock. Or if it is true, is that dumb or what? I mean, Sam was nice to me after the Finn shipwreck, but who could think that acting like a jerk was going to give me some idea to keep away from Finn? Nina, I'm not a little kid. I have ideas of my own. And I wasn't born yesterday. I mean, I know I was devastated by Finn—that jerk—but who told Sam to put on a play for me? And like I want his opinion anyway? I'm telling you, I was so mad at him. He is such a liar. And such a child! And to think, I might have liked him! Trust me, Nina, you're not the stupid one. Me neither. *They're* the stupid ones. Men. Or in Sam's case, little boys."

Nina looked thoughtful. "I don't know, Elizabeth," she said. "It sounds kind of sweet."

"Ha!" Elizabeth spat out. "If it even happened like that. I don't know what to think about anything he says. How can you trust a liar?"

Nina shook her head. "So what are you going to do?"

"About what?"

"Sam."

"Sam? Nothing. Kick him out of the duplex. Pretend we never met."

Nina took Elizabeth's hands in hers. Her voice was tentative. "Elizabeth? Are you sure you want to do that? I mean, maybe he lied about his past. And maybe he was sleeping with this Anna, or maybe he wasn't— but it sounds like he was trying to look out for you."

Elizabeth started to protest. "Who needs it—"

Nina cut her off with a raised finger. "But that's not the main thing. Look at yourself. Worrying about him. Driving all over town. Freaking out when you think he might be with another girl. Blowing up when you see you've been deceived. I don't think you just think you might have liked him. I think you like him. I think you might like him a lot. You guys have a lot of talking to do, and he's going to have to regain your trust, but—well, it doesn't take a rocket scientist to see that if you cut him out of your life, you're going to regret it."

Elizabeth tried to interject, but Nina held up her hand.

"Look, you're going to spend a long time wondering what might have happened if you'd given him a chance to make it up to you. You don't get so involved when you don't care. You do care. Admit it. You care a lot."

Elizabeth stared at her friend in amazement. Where had she come from, this angel? *Of course,* she thought, *she's right. Sam is impossible and a royal pain in the neck, but I can't forget about him. I couldn't if I tried.* She didn't say anything, though. She just felt the warmth of Nina's hands on hers. She was chagrined over her maternal feelings toward Nina. For someone who didn't have a lot of experience with guys, she had seen right through Elizabeth's huffing over Sam, right through to what was at the heart of it all: She cared about Sam. A lot. She had to admit it.

Nina smiled sweetly at Elizabeth's silence and took a sip of her coffee. Elizabeth was thinking about friends. *This is what it's all about,* she mused. *What we're here for.*

Nina looked up at the clock and said, "Hey, the movie Josh and I were going to see is starting in ten minutes. Wanna go?"

"What is it?"

"Hitchcock. *The Man Who Knew Too Much.*"

"A man who knew *too much*? This I've got to see. I can't imagine one even knowing nearly enough."

Laughing, they made their way to the door.

Chapter Fourteen

Jessica and Neil walked into Yum-Yum's together. After Neil's cryptic phone call with Jason, she was dying to find out what he had to "explain" to them. Both of them scanned the sparsely crowded coffee place, but there was no sign of Jason yet. They walked up to the counter and perused the menu posted on the wall.

"So, oat muffin and green tea for you?" Jessica playfully addressed Neil.

"I think I'll skip the cinder block and just get the puddle water. How 'bout you? Your usual double-fudge brownie and mochaccino, or are you still trying to maintain appearances?"

"I don't want to spoil my appetite. I think I'll stick with the green tea too, out of respect for Jason."

Neil turned to the goateed guy behind the counter. "Two green teas, please."

Jessica and Neil took their seats at a table for four and waited for Jason to arrive. It didn't take long before he appeared in the entrance and walked self-consciously to their table. He had traded his charcoal jeans for black ones and was wearing the same black T-shirt. He also had a lightweight black jacket with the zipper open. Jessica wondered silently if he were mourning something or just trying to look somber for whatever news he had to break to her and Neil.

Jessica got up from the table and gave Jason a quick kiss on the cheek. "Hi, Jason."

Neil got up too and shook Jason's hand in what Jessica couldn't help notice was a pretty stilted, formal gesture. "Hey, Jason, how's it going?"

Neil and Jessica both took their seats again, but Jason remained standing.

Neil looked up at him and gestured toward the empty chair between them. "Please, sit down."

"Yeah, take a load off," Jessica added, trying to keep the mood light, "and while you're at it, why don't you take off your coat and stay awhile?" *God,* Jessica said to herself. *Did that come out of my mouth? I sound like my father or something.*

Jason took the seat but kept his jacket on. He smiled awkwardly at her and then at Neil. "So, I guess you must be wondering why I've gathered you here today," he began, making his own little attempt at lightening the mood. "Well, like I said on the phone to Neil, this isn't very easy for me. But I thought it was best if I talk to you both together. I know you guys are best friends, and I know I've caused a lot of friction between the two of you, and, well, I just want to clear everything up. Before I cause any more problems."

Jessica was already beginning to think that she'd made the right decision when she told Neil that she wasn't going to go after Jason anymore. She could tell that whatever he had to say wasn't going to bode well for any kind of future between him and her. But whatever it was, she was ready to hear it.

"So, what's going on?" Jessica asked, hoping he would get to the point already.

"Okay, Jessica," he began, looking her directly in the eye, "first of all—and I hope you don't take this the wrong way, and I hope it doesn't bother you for me to say this in front of Neil—I never should have kissed you yesterday. Like I said on the phone to Neil, that was a big mistake."

Jessica crinkled her face in a combination of confusion and mild disgust and shot Neil a quick glance. *Funny Neil forgot to mention that part of the conversation,* she mused.

Turning back to face Jason, she asked him directly, "And why was it such a mistake? Because Neil walked in on us while it was happening?"

"No!" Jason blurted out. "I mean, yes, that was unfortunate. And I wish Neil didn't have to see that because the last thing I ever wanted to do was to hurt him—to hurt either of you. But that's not why it was a mistake. . . ." Jason hesitated before continuing.

"Go on," Jessica urged him impatiently.

"I guess I was sort of using you, Jessica," Jason admitted.

"What!" Jessica snapped.

"Well, um, what I mean is, I think I was using you to see if I could prove to myself that I wasn't really gay."

"What?" Neil piped up from across the table. "You mean, you *are* gay?"

"Well, yes," Jason answered reluctantly. "I mean, I think I am. . . . Yes, I am. But I wasn't sure until very, very recently. And I just thought that if I could, you know, be attracted to a girl, then maybe I could prove myself wrong about being homosexual. I'm pretty confused about the whole thing, as you can tell."

Jessica noticed Neil frowning across the table. In empathy, she guessed.

"So, you're *not* attracted to me," Jessica stated bluntly, and immediately hated herself for trying to make this whole conversation about her.

"Listen, Jessica, don't take this personally,"

Jason pleaded. "The reason I even pursued you in the first place is because you're the most beautiful girl on campus, and I figured if I could be attracted to any female that it must be you."

Jessica hated to admit it, but her ego was momentarily assuaged.

"And I'm sorry, Jessica, I really am. I'm sorry I dragged you through this. But I wouldn't have done it if I hadn't thought that there was some remote chance that things might work out between us. I never wanted to hurt your feelings, and there's really no reason you should feel bad about this."

Jessica nodded in acceptance and turned to look at Neil, who had a sort of stunned yet hopeful look on his face. She hoped that Jason would follow her cue and say whatever it was he needed to say to Neil.

"Which brings me to you, Neil." Jason now shifted his attention to the other side of the table. "First just let me apologize for dragging you through all of this too. But like I said, this has been a really difficult time for me. I've had a lot of confusion, a lot of questions."

Neil nodded and let Jason continue without interrupting.

"And the truth is, I really like you, Neil. And I can tell you like me too—that is, you did until yesterday. But I can't help thinking I've led you on, just like I was leading Jessica on."

"What do you mean?" Neil asked.

"What I mean, is, well . . . . ," Jason continued uncertainly. "Of course I knew that you were gay all along, but the way I was behaving toward you, it was almost like I was pretending you weren't or that I didn't know you were. And I think part of that was just a way of protecting myself—until I was sure about myself."

"So now that you *are* sure . . ." Neil paused suggestively.

Jason could evidently tell what Neil was getting at and struggled with his response. "I'm just sorry I didn't meet you at another time in my life. Because I really do like you. And the truth is, I'm attracted to you too. . . ."

"But?" Neil prompted him.

"But this just isn't the right time for me, Neil, and I'm sorry." Jason shook his head. "Like I said, I'm really just now coming to terms with my homosexuality. And I'm just not at a point yet where I feel like I can get involved with anyone. And I can tell that you're in a totally different space right now. I can tell that you are just so ready to fall in love with someone, and . . . well, I just hope you find someone who's better for you than I am right now. And I'm sure you will."

Jessica nearly started sobbing as she looked across the table at Neil, rubbing his forehead and pushing his hand roughly back and forth through his hair. A look of anguish consumed his face, and Jessica could tell that the reason he wasn't speaking was because he was afraid of crying. She'd thought *she* felt bad when Jason told her he wasn't attracted to her, but watching him break the news to Neil was ten times more painful.

"Well, you guys, I hope I didn't mess up your evening too badly," Jason announced as he abruptly pushed his chair back from the table. "And I'm sure that neither one of you wants anything to do with *me* right now, but, um, well, you never know. Maybe someday we can all be friends."

"Sure," Neil managed to say, with barely a hint of malice in his voice. He reached across the table to shake Jason's hand. "Take care of yourself, okay, man? And listen, if you ever need anyone to talk to about stuff, just give me a call, okay? I know how difficult all this can be."

Jason shook Neil's hand warmly and held on for a lingering moment. "Thanks, Neil. You take care too. And Jessica, you do the same. Really, thank you both for being so understanding."

Jason slowly rose to his feet. "Well, I guess this is good-bye."

"Bye, Jason," Jessica and Neil answered in unison.

As Jason walked out of Yum-Yum's, both Jessica

and Neil got to their feet at the same time. And without words, for the third time that day, they embraced. Jessica had never thought a hug that had nothing to do with making out could feel so good. Once again she just felt happy that she had a friend like Neil.

"Well," Neil announced as they stepped away from each other, "I guess we never have to eat another Yum-Yum's oat muffin again, eh, Jessica?"

"You got that right," Jessica agreed with a smile.

And then they went dancing.

Sam sat on the top step to the duplex. His butt was asleep, and the bouquet of flowers beside him seemed to be wilting. Sam looked up at the sky as dusk was falling and wondered if Elizabeth was ever going to return.

He had been on the porch for hours, insistent on seeing Elizabeth the moment she got home. He wanted to exhibit some kind of dedication to clearing the air between them, and waiting outside for her had seemed like the way to do it. Now he wasn't so sure. It was getting dark, and he was starting to think she had left town or something.

But he was afraid to go inside. Not even to grab a glass of water or go to the bathroom. If she came home while he was in the house, he was afraid it would mean that his hours on the porch had been wasted.

Then he saw her. She looked a lot better than she had last night, huddled in her bed and screaming at him. That was for sure. As he watched her from a distance, walking up the block, he saw a spring in her stride that was almost encouraging. Like she wasn't in such bad shape after all, even with all he had put her through this past week. She kept her eyes glued to the ground.

As she got closer, approaching the front steps, Sam was stunned at how beautiful she looked. Suddenly his hours on the porch were all worthwhile. To see her now, with the sun fading below the horizon, was absolutely magical. And he realized just how strong his feelings for her really were.

But as she mounted the stairs in front of the house and noticed Sam sitting there, her entire disposition changed. Her confident posture stiffened, and her determined smile became a look of disgust. Or was it pity? No, definitely disgust. Sam did feel pitiful, but Elizabeth didn't register any signs of sympathy. He was just glad she didn't make an about-face at the sight of him and walk back down the stairs.

But even with the scowl that now consumed her features, the sight of her was absolutely breathtaking. He had spent so many endless hours trying to formulate what he would say to her when he saw her.

But now that she was before him, with all her beauty and poise—and not to forget, that look of animosity—every clear thought disappeared from his head.

Sam stood up awkwardly and walked down the steps to the base of the porch. He reached out with the lilies and irises as a peace offering, but Elizabeth made no attempt to accept them. She firmly crossed her arms over her chest and stared at Sam without saying anything.

"Elizabeth, I really need to talk to you."

"Hmmm."

"God, you don't know how long I've been waiting out here for you to come home," Sam blurted out.

"Oh, well, I'm so sorry," she answered acridly.

"N-No, that's not what I meant," he stammered. "I mean, I've been wanting to talk to you for so long, it's, like, now that you're finally here, I don't even know what to say."

Oh, great! Sam scolded himself. *This is going just great, isn't it? You wait for her to come home so you can tell her how much you want to be with her, and then you get on her case for being late?* What was he thinking?

"That's a good one, Sam. You disappear for four days, shacked up at the Sweet Valley Resort Hotel with your little girlfriend while I'm worried sick about you, driving all over town, making a fool out of myself in front of my friends and our housemates, and now it's *you* who's been wanting to talk to *me?*"

"Look, Elizabeth, I tried to explain all that to you last night, but you wouldn't listen. I'm the one who's sucking it up to talk to you again, okay, so maybe you should—"

Elizabeth's eyes narrowed. "Oh, *I* should? I don't think *I* should do anything where you're concerned, Burgess. You know, I've had a really long day, and all I really want to do right now is go inside and lie down for a while. So, if you'll excuse me, I'd rather not have this conversation right now. And I especially don't want to have it outside, in front of the house."

"Fine," he said. "So that's it. You're not even going to listen to me. I'm ready to talk to you now, Liz."

"Yeah, *right,* Sam. Whenever *you're* ready. That's the way it always has to be with you, doesn't it? You say what you want to say *when you want to say it.* Never mind what other people think or feel. Never mind that I didn't ask you to wait for me to get home just for you to give me another little song-and-dance routine. Never mind that I told you last night that I want you out of my life."

Now Sam was completely flustered. "Elizabeth, please, wait. Just let me talk, okay?"

"No, not okay. You've had plenty of chances to talk, Sam. And the only things that have come out of your mouth are lies. Pitiful excuses and lies. And you have no right to ambush me here in the front yard with your pathetic little bouquet just because you finally feel like talking. Just because you're finally ready to tell the truth or whatever your version of the truth happens to be today. You know, Sam, everyone was right about you. You are the most arrogant, selfish, deceitful human being I have ever had the *dis*pleasure of knowing. I am so *over* you!"

Elizabeth pushed by Sam and scurried up the steps. Sam followed close behind, but by the time he made it to the porch, Elizabeth was already through the door, which she promptly slammed in his face. Before he had a chance to feel hurt by her rejection, anger consumed Sam's entire being. And every wall that he had carefully built up inside himself, every facade that he had finally begun to chip away at over these past few days, were all instantly resurrected. And Sam the sham was back again.

That's just fine, Sam insisted to himself. *I never needed her anyway. And she never needed me, either. Who says I needed to level with her anyway? I don't care about the truth. I can be anyone I want to be. It's better this way.*

Much better. Now I can go back to being my old obnoxious self and do what I please. Yeah, and kiss Elizabeth Wakefield good-bye forever.

Check out the **all-new**....

(Sweet Valley Web site—)

www.sweetvalley.com

New Features

Cool Prizes

The **ONLY** official Web site!

Hot Links

(And much more!)